LOVE ME

tomorrow

ETHAN DAY

LOVE ME
tomorrow

Janice –
Thank you so much
for joining us in KC!
I hope you had an
amazing weekend!!
Much love
Ethan Day

ETHAN DAY

WILDE CITY
PRESS

WILDE CITY PRESS

www.wildecity.com

Love Me Tomorrow © 2015 Ethan Day

Published in the US and Australia by Wilde City Press 2015

Published by Wilde City Press

ISBN: 978-1-925180-76-3

Cover Art © 2015 Wilde City Press

ACKNOWLEDGEMENTS

I'd like to thank the following people for helping me get this book completed and ready for release.

Thank you to Stephani Hecht, Lisa Edwards & Hannah for your help with all things paramedical.

To Jambrea Jo Jones—book-title-giver and beta-speed-reader extraordinaire—many thanks for once again appeasing my neurosis by reassuring me that I don't suck, lol.

My eternal gratitude to Ally Blue who has helped me with all things medical over the years, from Boone & Wade to Fox & Tucker to Levi & Jake. I can't thank you enough for having generously given your time over multiple years and multiple books—your friendship and support is greatly appreciated.

Further thanks to Lisa Edwards for your support and attention to detail over multiple manuscripts and for always letting me know when I've made you laugh!

To JP Bowie who has been an incredible friend and supporter since our first meeting back in 2010, many thanks for helping me write this book by imparting some of your own wisdom and personal history. Next drink is on me, Dewar's Lad!

To Kris Jacen, who has assisted me in bringing so many wildly fun and entertaining characters to life across the pages of multiple books—there are a great many things I have likely never fully thanked you enough for over the years and for that I am truly sorry. In the event I've never said it before, many thanks for always being there, beyond your work as an editor, with a kind word, a sympathetic ear and the occasional offering of friendly advice. You have been an incredible friend and you are much loved.

Finally, my heartfelt gratitude to anyone and everyone out there for purchasing and reading my books. I cannot ever fully put into words what that means to me, so I will simply say, thank you.

CHAPTER ONE

"A little to the right, please." Levi Goode took several steps backward as the two men on ladders shifted the eight by six foot canvas backdrop featuring a vintage Carnival-themed bearded lady, wearing a Victorian era costume including all the frills and ruffles. It was the last of nearly eighty in total showcasing various Carnival-themed attractions of yesteryear which now hung throughout the tent.

"That's it, right there—that is perfect guys, thank you so much."

They nodded their appreciation for the gratitude and the younger, hunkier one of the two dramatically sighed his relief as he started down the ladder.

Levi let it roll off his back, aware he'd been a bit a tyrant the past few days. He wasn't typically this high-strung, but his stress level had been at DEFCON Five for weeks and it had begun to make him a little rough around the edges. He had gambled his entire reputation, not to mention a small chunk of his own savings, on this one event. His entire future hung in the balance and this one night was a make or break moment for his business, Goode City Event & Party Planning.

All in all, he was currently in charge of wrangling hundreds of volunteers, not including his own people and all the staff from the catering company. Beyond that, were the entertainers and a small army of service staff that had been hired—the bartenders and waiters—to work the event, serving the over nine hundred guests who had paid upwards of $2500 a plate to attend tonight's benefit.

Surveying the monstrous three-ring circus sized tent which stood nearly four stories high at the tallest peak, Levi made mental check-marks on the forever-long list inside his head: the portable bars scattered throughout were all set up and ready for service; the pristine tablecloths covering the tables; and the elegant centerpieces were being put into place.

They had hours to go, yet the amount of work that was still left to do felt insurmountable. The stage appeared to be alive, now crawling with roadies and technicians setting up for the big band orchestra. Everything was coming together and Levi was cautious and excited and…

"…scared shitless all at the same time."

Chastising himself for using profanity, Levi sighed, thinking it was already October and he was still struggling to remove that language from his vocabulary. It was the lone New Year's resolution he'd made for 2014 and considering the year was almost over, it was beginning to feel a bit futile.

He decided to cut himself some slack, deciding it was the stress talking.

The culmination of the past nine months' worth of planning and hard work was only a few hours away and despite his somewhat frayed nerves, Levi was certain it would all pay off in the end—it's what he kept telling himself at any rate. The Cancer Prevention Charity Ball was one of *the* influential society events in Wilde City each year and had raised millions of dollars in the past. This was the first year in over a decade that the event planning had been opened up to outside bidding.

Until her collapse from a heart attack at the Silverman-Bingley wedding last winter, event planner Libby Washington had enjoyed a decade-long stranglehold over any and all of the major society events in Wilde City. She was a ruthless woman, so diabolical, that anyone who attempted to venture out and hire anyone else wound up regretting it.

Everyone feared Libby, and rightfully so, as her vengeance was legendary. Restaurants she deemed worthy of her benevolence, that turned around and worked with any other party planners, found themselves shut down due to health code violations. Hotels that didn't give her priority over event space rentals suffered horrible reviews and rumors of bed bugs, shingles outbreaks and the like. Then there was legendary, long-time and well-beloved Mayor Frances, considered to be a shoo-in for re-election several years back, who found himself voted out of office when he had the gall to ask a family member to organize his inaugural gala.

Libby was still a force, in spite of the heart attack that nearly claimed her life all those months ago. However, a crack in her armor had been exposed and she no longer had the pull she once did. The fact it had been medically confirmed that she actually had a heart had been her undoing, so to speak. Everyone she'd ever intimidated or bullied into subservience was now all too willing to step over her bloodied corpse.

"You reap what you sow," Levi mumbled to himself as he scrolled down the itinerary on his tablet, checking to ensure things were ticking along as intended.

The only damper on the evening's event was the fact Libby was expected to attend the gala—the one dark stain on the horizon that no amount of scrubbing could possibly alleviate. Levi had hired outside security as a result. It would be just like her to attempt some sort of sabotage. He couldn't keep that hag from coming to the party, but he could damn well make sure she remained under constant surveillance while she was inside his tent.

Someone really needs to drop a house on that witch.

Levi winced at the shriek of a microphone sound check gone wrong. His phone began chirping, as did several others around him. He then noticed bells chiming and ringtones were going off all throughout the tent. He began reaching for his own phone when he heard several whooping sounds being shouted all around him. His curiosity evaporated the instant he saw his assistant, Valerie, running toward him at a breakneck pace.

Something was terribly wrong and Levi's chest began to tighten, making it difficult to breathe.

What I get for thinking bad thoughts about demon-Libby.

"Levi Goode," Caroline Sparks called out, her sweetly seductive voice all but licking the stress away as she strode toward him with a huge smile on her face. "I knew hiring you was the right call. Just look at this place!"

He took a very brief moment to glance around, double checking for any fires, imagined or otherwise, that needed to be put out. Then her words sank in, and he realized her smile combined with the phrase 'right call' were positives.

"Thank you, Caroline. I'm so happy you're pleased."

The caterer had told him that Caroline had pushed for him to get the contract; that made him especially keen to see she was happy with his services. She'd been on the city council since the late eighties and was well-respected amongst the community. Dressed in a grey pant suit, she looked like a politician—well-pressed and professionally coiffed—though Levi had never picked up any indications that she was anything less than sincere.

She'd no doubt stopped by to check in on his progress on her way home from work.

He noticed two of the bartenders on the other side of the tent high-fiving one another as people's cell phones continued to chirp and bleep all around them. Valerie was now standing at his side and looked like she was about to explode.

"Pleased?" Caroline said, looking around the space. "I'm practically gleaming. It's just beautiful, stunning, really, Levi, it's more than I'd even hoped for."

He let out a little sigh and she reached over and gave his arm a squeeze.

"Not for nothing and despite the fact I'm fully aware it's not polite to speak ill of the dead, I have to say that you, my boy, are so much easier to deal with than that dreadful Libby Washington."

It took several seconds and seeing Valerie completely deflate before the words sunk in. "Libby passed away?" The reason behind the phone bleeping and chirping became clear. Word of Libby's demise was making the rounds and the people who'd suffered under her reign over the past ten years were apparently ready to celebrate.

Caroline smiled evilly while nodding her head. "Which means my *very* good friend, Julia Freeman-Kingsley, will be in *desperate* need of a new party planner for her annual anniversary bash in December."

Levi's mouth fell open and Valerie let out a tiny squeak. Snagging a senator's daughter as a new client would be quite the coup.

"I'll make sure Julia manages to find you later this evening." Caroline began walking away, nodding politely at Valerie. Then she began spinning around in a circle and giggling like a little girl. "You're a revelation, Mr. Goode, I just love it—I love everything."

"That one needs to adjust her medication," Valerie blurted, the instant Caroline was out of earshot.

Levi shot her a nasty look and she smiled up at him.

Valerie was at least a foot shorter than his six-foot frame, with pale skin and hair dyed black as night, styled in that retro Betty-Page-with-bangs kind of way. She had a dangerously curvy physique and she enjoyed wearing borderline inappropriately tight clothing.

The woman enjoyed walking the line of propriety. She was an excellent assistant, able to forecast his needs typically before Levi was even aware he needed something, but she had the absolute worst attitude. It wasn't that she was negative so much as bawdy—though she managed to ensure Levi was the only witness to her brazen behavior.

Lucky me.

"I'm sorry, it's not natural for anyone to be that happy," Valerie added in her defense, watching Caroline walking off.

"You should be nicer considering she is single-handedly responsible for ensuring you'll continue to receive a paycheck as we move into the New Year." Levi pulled his phone out and tapped the button so it would stop chirping at him. As suspected, there were a slew of texts about Libby's passing, from his mother and several acquaintances within the local hospitality industry. "Plus, if we land the Freeman-Kingsley gig, I'll be able to hire more staff."

Valerie gasped, clasping her hands together like she was ready to pray—an act Levi assumed she'd been otherwise unfamiliar with before that day.

"I've always wanted underlings," she said in a hushed, breathy voice. A somewhat sadistic expression stole over her face and Levi began to fear the monster he was about to create. "Minions," she added, using a creepy whisper while tapping her fingertips together and looking particularly wicked.

He smacked at her hands fearing she might frighten the rest of the herd and Valerie laughed, no doubt pleased she'd been able to get a rise out of him.

That seemed to be her life's mission.

"You are so uptight, Levi," Valerie stated, disappointment evident in her voice. "I'm going to find a horse-hung waiter for you to take home at the end of the night."

"That's an exceedingly inappropriate thing to say to your employer," Levi reminded her.

"Fortunately for me, we're also friends," she said, matter-of-factly. "I'm one of the very few you have."

"I have plenty of friends!"

"Please." She shook her head. "People you do business with, who you also happen to be friendly with? Not even remotely the same thing."

"So you're saying I'm friendless?"

"Except for me? Yeah, pretty much."

"That doesn't feel true."

"Oh, but it is," she insisted

"Better keep me away from razor blades and bridges then."

"You don't have to get all melodramatic. All I'm saying is I'm the only one who is trying to get you laid."

"Which isn't humiliating in the least, like I'm some charity case you need to run around procuring sexual favors for?"

"Kinda, yeah."

"Oh my God, that's so mean." Levi stared at her, waiting for the 'I'm just kidding' that never came. "Allow me to run back up to the bell tower where I belong."

"You're not ugly, Levi, in fact, you're a bit of a boy-babe with the enticingly thick, totally-touchable, dark hair and long, lanky bod. Unfortunately, you're also boring—"

"Not really making me feel better."

"—and a little lame, but that's the worst of it."

"Wow!"

She gave his butt a pat. "You do have a totally fuckable tight little ass, though."

"So…I'm like cardboard with a warm hole? Thank you for that two-dimensional assessment of my personality."

"You're quite welcome," she said, as if the gratis he'd offered had been sincere.

Levi sneered. "That being said, I'll stick with finding my own dates, if it's all the same to you."

"Fine, be that way. You're utterly hopeless. I'll just buy you some cats and call it a day."

"Wha—"

She stomped off in a huff, not waiting around for a response.

"Rude!" he called out after her, then glanced around realizing people were now staring at him.

Levi shrugged it off and went back to his checklist, smiling at the hunky waiter that walked by with a uniform slung over his well-muscled shoulder, while wondering if he was into cardboardy warm-holed men.

Bad, bad-bad! Do not follow Valerie into her twisted rabbit hole from hell.

Someday my freakin' prince will come, goddamn it, he reminded himself.

Walt freakin' Disney couldn't have said it better.

He nodded as he headed off in the direction of the sound stage, reminding himself that until that time there was always work... blessed work.

* * * *

From the funhouse mirror-lined entryway that led into the big top, to the fire breathers and sword swallowers that followed the five-star, four-course cuisine which had been painstakingly selected by both Levi and local celebrity, Chef Margo, and finally the burlesque scarf acrobats who had just finished performing to an ear deafening round of applause, the entire evening had gone off without a hitch.

The big band had kicked into high gear and the torch singer was crooning away as people began heading toward the dance floor.

"Cue the Carnival," Levi whispered into his Bluetooth.

Within an instant, the entire back wall of the tent fell away, revealing several brightly lit carnival rides all decked out in golden-white lights. The squeals and gasps followed by another round of resounding applause was what he'd been hoping for. He'd kept things simple: a giant Ferris wheel, a huge carousel, some sort of Egyptian-themed pendulum-like boat ride, a wacky house with a maze and moving floors and a giant slide that utilized felt sleds.

It was a black tie affair, and he was aware there were a good many in attendance that wouldn't be caught dead zipping down a giant slide in their best red carpet evening gown or tux. However, just as he'd hoped, seeing a rush of partygoers head outside toward the carnival rides, there were enough who'd had just enough wine with dinner to have forgotten themselves long enough to try.

A return to childhood.

It was more for the effect than anything else, and thankfully, despite the cold snap in the weather they'd experienced during the first part of the month, the early October temperature had held on beautifully. It was a little chilly but hanging in there right around the upper-sixties.

The Ferris wheel alone was worth a ride, taking people up high enough to get a lovely view of the water and the entire boardwalk all lit up. Bottom line, this event would be talked about for months and with any luck, Goode City Event's phone would be ringing off the hook for the foreseeable future. This type of exposure with this kind of clientele was priceless. It was why he'd offered his services at no charge… well that, and the whole warm n' fuzzy feeling that accompanied the cancer fundraising aspect.

"This must be Merlin," a man's voice said from behind him.

Levi turned, grinning at Caroline who'd made good on her promise to introduce him to Julia Freeman-Kingsley and her husband, Gregory Kingsley, whose family owned a slew of paper mills and printing companies around the globe.

"Please, call me Gregory." He offered his hand, which Levi accepted. "I had to come and meet the maestro responsible for this production. I'm still waiting for the movie cameras to pop out, Spielberg."

Gregory Kingsley had that old-school, matinee idol look about him. He was sexy-pretty with a little gleam in his eye like he might be ready to pull a prank at a moment's notice. His dark blond wavy hair was combed back all neat and shiny, not a hair out of place. However, it was the perpetually present sarcastic looking smirk that pushed the man over the edge, making him nearly borderline-irresistible.

"Thank you, Gregory, that's very kind of you to say." Levi was gleeful over the indulgent compliments offered by Kingsley, despite his best attempts to otherwise control himself. "I sincerely hope everyone is enjoying themselves."

"You had my husband with the hooch," Julia said, shaking Levi's hand as well.

"The wine selection *was* amazing," Gregory added.

Levi laughed, thinking he instantly liked Mr. Kingsley, easy to please and quick with a compliment. His wife had trained him well.

"When you plan our anniversary gala I'll expect the same production level," Julia said with a wink.

He prayed that the wink indicated she was kidding.

"I'll leave you to it," Caroline said, waving as she scurried off toward the dance floor.

"Caroline has been raving about you all evening," Julia said.

"Oh, well, that's ni—"

"Since our anniversary is in December," Gregory said, cutting Levi off mid-pleasantry, "we were thinking shirtless, sexy Santa servers for the ball-and-chain here and Thunderdome-style elf mud wrestling for me."

"You idiot, ignore him, please." Julia playfully punched her husband on the chin. "He's obviously sampled *too much* of the wine selection."

Dressed elegantly in a glistening, floor-length silver gown that clung to her thin frame, Julia looked like a shimmering goddess. He wasn't sure what the fabric was made of, but she practically twinkled as light reflected off the material. Her long, dark brown hair cascaded in soft curls, meticulously styled in a 1940s Hollywood-glam inspired hairdo. Her voice had that crisp New England sounding tone that reminded him of Katherine Hepburn or a Kennedy and Levi found himself slightly mesmerized by her.

She looked much lovelier in person than in the photographs from the newspaper society pages. "I recognize that look all too well," Gregory said, glancing over at his wife. "If he weren't gay you'd have to find a different party planner."

"I'm sorry, I didn't mean to stare." Levi felt his face flush with heat.

"It's sweet that he still gets jealous after all these years," Julia said, patting her husband on the chest. "Baby, why don't you go and play with your friends?"

"I know when I'm not wanted," he said with a sigh, reaching out to shake Levi's hand once more. "Look forward to hearing what you have planned for our party and don't dismiss the elf mud wrestling too quickly. The Freemans do so enjoy being the center of attention."

"Not that sort of attention, pal," she said, shoving him away as he laughed.

"Nice to meet you," Levi called out.

"He really is the worst, but I love the big lug," she said, taking Levi by the arm. "I realize you're no doubt preoccupied at the moment, but I didn't want to waste a minute as your phone will no doubt be ringing off the hook come tomorrow morning. I simply had to get my foot in the door before anyone else."

"Obviously, I'd be thrilled to work with you, Mrs. Freeman-Kingsley, and I—"

"Julia, please, call me Julia," she insisted, giving his arm a squeeze as she began walking and pulling him along. "Unfortunately, my anniversary has been turned into quite a production over the years. It's despicable, really, but Daddy has a terrible time hearing the word 'no'. The evening has a tendency to become more about feeding the all-consuming political beast of Father's career."

"Happy anniversary to you," Levi said, sarcastically, then wished he hadn't been quite so informal.

She grinned, much to his relief. "You already get me, I can tell."

He smiled nodding. "So it will be my mission to provide you and your husband with a much needed shot of romance to go along with all the political pageantry."

"Good luck," Julia scoffed, tossing in a roll of her eyes for good measure. "I gave up on that eons ago. Allow me to further burst your sweet and completely adorable fantasy-romance bubble by offering you some free advice. Never get married at Christmas time, because all of the relatives you hate show up like the ghosts of Christmas past… then proceed to shit all over everything. It's a real mood-killer. Bad enough they had to be at the actual wedding, you know? It's like signing up for an annual anniversary straight from the bowels of Hell."

She smirked, seemingly pleased by the expression of shock on his face that he'd apparently not done a very good job at hiding.

"Don't get me wrong, I adore my husband and would marry him again in an instant—"

"Just not in December?" Levi asked.

"Exactly!" Julia nodded, glancing down at his hands. "Do you have a partner?"

Levi blinked, taking a beat, thinking it slightly odd she had asked or would even care, and found it mildly unsettling that she and her husband knew he was even gay. "Nope, no time really."

"Pish!" She smacked him gently in the arm. "You make time for love, young man. It may not be legal across the country…yet… but the piece of paper does not make the marriage."

"Still, it doesn't suck to have it, I would imagine," Levi said.

"We'll get there, one day." She sighed as they continued to stroll along the exterior of the tent, avoiding any eavesdroppers. "My twin brother is gay and he's the single best person I've ever known."

Levi vaguely recalled that fact, remembering the photos of a teenaged Julia and her brother splashed all over the newspapers during election years throughout the nineties. But it had been a long time since Levi had heard anything about Julia's twin.

He smiled, seeing she'd gone quiet. "Odd that your father would be so against gay marriage when he has a gay son."

She rolled her eyes.

"God, I'm so sorry, I can't believe I just said that out loud."

Julia once again appeared to take pleasure from his squirming. "There wasn't a hint of judgment in your voice, so please don't fret, Levi. It's something I've never been able to wrap my own brain around either."

They continued to stroll along, though Julia had apparently drifted off into her own thoughts. Levi decided to leave her be and let her come back when she was ready.

"Apologies," Julia finally blurted out, letting go of his arm. "Didn't mean to digress so far off the topic."

"Not a problem."

She nodded, opening her clutch, digging out a sterling silver business card holder which had her initials engraved on the lid.

"This card has my personal cell number and will get you past my assistant, though her contact information is also listed there. I'd like to meet with you very soon, like within the next week, if possible, while tonight's events are still fresh in my parents' minds."

Levi nodded, taking the card from her and slipping it into the inside pocket of his tuxedo jacket. It made sense of course, that he would have to pass inspection from the good senator, a fact he hadn't considered until that moment.

"Rest assured," she placed a hand on his arm, "I always get everything I want, but things will be ever-so-much easier if we get them on our side from the beginning."

Levi grinned, appreciating that she already viewed him as part of her team. He'd instantly liked everything about her, and did even more so now. So much so that he set his mind on providing her with some magic and romance during this party, whether she thought it possible or not. "Say no more, I am your willing accomplice and co-conspirator from this moment forward. You name it and I will find some way to make it happen."

"Never tell a girl like me something like that, Levi Goode." Julia started to walk away, then turned back and smiled playfully. "I might think you mean it."

* * * *

Levi slowly strode along the boardwalk, comforted by the sound of his shoes clicking along the thick wooden slats underfoot. The salty sea air seemed thicker, with a light fog beginning to roll in off the water. It was just after three a.m. and Levi had worked through his own exhaustion and was now entirely too slaphappy to go to bed. The event had gone off without a hitch and he had certainly reaped the rewards, he thought, patting his jacket pocket which was stuffed full of business cards from several of Wilde City's elite.

He'd decided to walk the few blocks back to his loft in hopes it would allow him time to decompress and come down off the high he was currently riding. However, his brain was already making lists on how to proceed over the next few days. He was picturing the graphs and pie charts, the prioritization of which potential new clients to contact first… the thought of being booked out for months, hell… perhaps even as much as a year or more?

He was in nerdy, overly-organizational heaven until remembering that Goode City was entirely too short staffed to handle the influx of new business. His smile faded slightly, but he quickly shrugged off the panic that was threatening to encroach upon his good cheer. He'd been collecting resumes for the past few months in preparation for this very moment. Plus with Libby's passing there was potential to poach some of her staff who'd been left unemployed with little notice.

His phone bleeped, alerting that him of a text message. Retrieving it from his pocket he smirked seeing it was from Valerie.

Stop obsessing and go 2 bed…u little freak.

He rolled his eyes, wondering why he put up with her rudeness.

The phone bleeped again.

Cuz I'm the only 1 who is completely honest with u. Go. 2. Bed.

His lip curled, hating it when she did that. It was like she could read his thoughts at times.

He decided to ignore her text completely, but noticed he had a voice mail. A few clicks and he placed the phone up to his ear.

"Levi, it's your mother, Ruby."

He shook his head, wondering why she felt the need to clarify that, as if he wouldn't have known otherwise.

"I just saw you on the nightly news!" she squealed. *"You look so handsome in your tuxedo, I nearly died! So proud... though I don't know why you had to mention that asshole Dan by name. Honestly, he treated you horribly and there you are on the news, promoting the bastard."*

"Tell me how you really feel, Mother," Levi muttered.

"Anyway, I wanted to say how proud I was of you and how handsome you looked. I know you'll be busy for the next few days so don't worry about me, love. And if you end up getting back together with that Dan Cain prick, I'll never speak to you again. Kisses!"

Levi sighed, thinking the fact she asked him not to, meant he needed to go check on her tomorrow night after work. It never ceased to amaze him that Ruby felt it her duty to continually pass judgment over his love life, or the lack thereof, considering her long and not-so-illustrious track record with men.

It dawned on him he was getting angry over nothing considering he was not getting back together with his most recent ex. They'd broken up because Levi had wanted more than Dan was capable of giving and Levi didn't see that fact changing any time soon.

He shook his head, attempting to force all of that unpleasantness from his brain, deciding to focus on anything else as he strode leisurely down the boardwalk. Caught up in a brisk breeze, Levi recalled the gasps and resounding applause that followed the reveal of the carnival rides earlier that evening and he smiled, then started laughing. He continued walking but spun around in a couple of circles, ala Mary Tyler Moore, wishing he had a hat to toss up into the air.

For the first time in a long time all the problems he had were good ones. That was a welcome blessing.

He turned, hearing a car slowing from behind him and it was as if his mother had conjured the man out of the encroaching fog merely by mentioning his name.

Dan's metallic silver Mercedes SLS convertible slowed, then pulled over toward the curb and rolled along as Levi continued walking—his way of not giving the man the impression he wanted to speak to him. Still, Levi plastered on a smile as Dan lowered the driver's side window because he didn't want the man to know that he harbored any ill will.

"You need a ride?" Dan asked.

Levi bent down to see the passenger side held Dan's current squeeze, the snotty, steroided-twink that he suspected Dan had dumped him for. His name was Kevin and he was chattering away on his cell phone, acting as if no one else in the world existed.

"I don't need a lift, actually, enjoying the walk, though it doesn't look like there'd be any room even if I did."

"We could squeeze in," Dan said. "Kevin wouldn't mind."

Levi leaned over, taking another glance over at Kevin, who refused to even look at Levi.

"I'm good, Dan, thanks anyway."

"Okay, well I never got a chance to tell you earlier, but you did a fucking amazing job tonight, Levi. I was thoroughly impressed."

Levi nodded, trying not to stare into Dan's eyes for any length of time for fear he'd once again fall prey to the man's hypnotizing, evil gaze and forget all about the fact Dan was not the guy for him. It had been nearly two years since they'd split, and the man still managed to affect Levi in some sort of base, carnal-desire kind of way.

"Seriously, people will be talking about tonight for years. You truly outdid yourself. And I can't thank you enough for bringing all this attention and media focus down to the docks, Levi. I owe you."

"It was the right place for the event, Dan, so think nothing of it."

Dan nodded, seeming to sense that Levi didn't actually want anything else to do with him. "I won't forget it, that's all I'm saying."

Levi sighed, wishing things had turned out differently between the two of them. He'd never come out and asked Dan if he'd cheated, but Kevin had been working as a gopher/intern in Dan's office in the months leading up Levi's break-up with Dan, so the fact they started dating right after Dan and Levi split felt… too convenient.

"Well… congratulations again," Dan said. "Always knew you'd make a splash like this one day."

The only feelings he had left for Dan were various shades of regret. "Thanks Dan, you have a good night."

With that, Dan sped away, tail lights disappearing into the fog until there was no longer any trace the man had been there at all, aside from Levi's memories.

In truth, Levi didn't want to know if Dan had been cheating. He was well aware that he'd suffered a major blind spot where Dan was concerned—most likely because the sex had been phenomenal. He could feel himself getting hard as he walked along the boardwalk, recalling exactly how much he'd enjoyed it. But that sort of blind-lust meant Levi would have been more prone to overlook any signs that Dan might have been making a fool of him the entire time they'd been dating.

Growing up the way he had, with Ruby and her never ending merry-go-round of men who'd lied to her incessantly, telling her what she wanted to hear until it was time for them to cut and run—it all felt a little too close to home. Levi never thought of himself as the type to fall for the same type of man, but he was well aware that he suffered from trust issues as a result of Ruby's frenetic love life.

It hurt more somehow, knowing that Dan had always respected him on a professional level. The fact he could so easily drop someone he held in such high regard, somehow made it worse. Deep down, Levi understood that he couldn't ever be what Dan needed him to be. Dan liked to be in control—he liked younger guys who didn't necessarily know who they wanted to be. He wanted to have someone waiting on bended knee at the door when he got home, ready with a scotch on the rocks and a blow job.

Levi had been that guy when they first met, but not long after they started dating his own ambitions quickly began to take precedence over being Dan Cain's plaything. Beyond that, Levi understood that Dan was never going to be the man Levi needed him to be. Levi wanted a relationship—to find a partner he could settle down with.

Dan was incapable of commitment.

It hadn't been easy for Levi to reach out to him. The revitalization and restoration of the docks and boardwalk had cost the city a fortune. Even with how beautiful the area was now, there hadn't been a huge flock of businesses that had jumped at the chance to move into the area. There were still a lot of empty storefronts, mostly due to the lack of residential influx that had been forecasted when the city initially approved the project.

Unfortunately, coming off a recession, the price tag for most of the lofts, which currently sat on the market unsold, were beyond the average means of most people. To Dan's credit the lofts had been beautifully refurbished—the entire six block area had been stunningly restored, right down to the newly uncovered cobblestone streets and gaslight streetlamps which created a picturesque glow, as it did now with the fog rolling in off the water.

When he'd approached Dan about using the community boardwalk area as part of his pitch to the board of directors of the Cancer Gala committee, Dan jumped all over the idea, knowing all the extra press and focused publicity on the area could potentially pay off for him. It's how Levi managed to get the event space at no cost. The fact Levi was aware the historical tie-in to the location would appeal to the old-money society folks, who looked back fondly on the golden Gatsby-esque days of Wilde City, when their robber-baron ancestors made millions working people to death in sweat shops, hadn't escaped him.

What he hadn't expected was Dan's plea for Levi to set an example by moving his business to the area as well. In the past nine months, his entire life had been uprooted when he purchased two floors of an exquisitely restored building right on the waterfront. The top floor, which he jokingly referred to as the penthouse and the storefront on the main level of the four-story building had become both home and work.

He'd purchased both at a steeply reduced rate, which was still a lot of money to him. But the commute no longer sucked, which was a huge bonus.

He'd also taken a teensy bit of pleasure having Dan fall all over himself to make Levi an offer he'd been unable to refuse. A lot had changed in two years. Dan used to enjoy tossing his money around like it was nothing, but was now in quite the precarious financial state. Of course that fact had nothing to do with Levi's decision to stage the benefit from the newly refurbished boardwalk and docklands. That the area was still struggling to get back on its feet made it appealing financially, but beyond that, the setting was simply too good to pass up.

Back in the late 1800's, the original Le Carnaval de Rêves had opened along the pier and remained a popular tourist destination until the Great Depression hit in '29. In the years that followed the economic collapse, most of the businesses along the waterfront went under and much of the shipping industry dried up with the demise of Howard Hart's transportation empire. Not long after, the docklands became a rather seedy and unsavory place. The landscape of Wilde City had been different back in those days, prohibition, corrupt politicians and mobsters like Mama Marlow and Bugsy Brown cut a path of death and destruction, terrorizing the entire city.

Levi imagined it all as being very *Sin City*.

Of course it was all completely romanticized nowadays, but from the research he'd done while putting together a prospectus for the Cancer Benefit, it was a bloody time in Wilde City history that he was personally happy to have missed.

Not that Levi suffered under the impression there wasn't plenty of corruption floating around just underneath the surface these days. The powers-that-be were cleaning up the city one borough at a time, slapping on a fresh coat of paint and charging a small fortune as the price of admission for the privilege to live there. He'd witnessed one or two shady dealings during the time he'd dated Dan and had turned a blind eye—payoffs and the like, greasing the palms of those who could push along permits—stuff like that.

The price of doing business, he'd assumed. Levi sighed, thinking he'd paid a price for his own success as well.

He'd done his best to ignore that longing inside which he'd been attempting to outrun over the last year or so. Even now, Levi tried in vain to ignore that fact, in spite of any accomplishments he'd experienced earlier that evening. It was tempered by the undeniable fact he was lonely— desperately so at times. Valerie had him pegged on that one, even though Levi didn't believe her recommendations that random sex would truly fix what ailed him. A Band-Aid perhaps, but a solution, sex was not.

He ached for a sort of soul-altering connection to go along with any earth-shattering orgasms. While he was certainly proud of all he'd accomplished, not having anyone special to share it with created a none-too-pleasant stabbing sensation in his chest.

Levi glanced both directions, squinting through the fog, straining to make sure no headlights could be spotted from oncoming traffic before he stepped off the boardwalk and sprinted across the road to his brand new home at 219 Waterfront Drive.

A problem for another day, he told himself, forcing any sadness or regret back down where it belonged while digging through his pockets for his keys. He began to feel the sting from want or need of sleep behind his eyes.

"Be it ever so humble, there's no place like home."

CHAPTER TWO

Making the sharp turn into Honeymoon Hills, Levi waved at the firemen as he passed the fire engine that was exiting the sprawling park-like subdivision which sat on over a hundred acres. He yawned, placing his triple-espresso-multi-caramel-pumped Starbucks back into the cup holder of the Prius, wishing the caffeine would hurry up and kick in already. As expected, the entire workday had been spent fielding calls and returning messages that had come pouring in since the Cancer benefit the night before.

Located inland, about forty minutes outside the city, Downham Parish was part of the Southwestern borough that had gained popularity in the early 1900s as more people began fleeing the city in an attempt to escape the crime and corruption.

Honeymoon Hills had been developed throughout the 1920s and 30s, architecturally comprised of mostly American bungalows—Craftsmans and Tudors mainly, but there was also a smattering of other styles tossed in to break up the monotony. The homes sat atop lush treed lots featuring soft rolling hills and were now prized and very sought after. Not so much when Levi and Ruby relocated to the area after fleeing Las Vegas back in the early nineties, but a lot had changed over the past twenty years. It was now a popular area for those who desired the best of both worlds, the beauty of Mother Nature combined with homes that had charm and character.

For Levi, moving to Downham Parish had been a welcome change from life in Las Vegas. It was one of those double-edged situations for him. On the one hand he knew Ruby would have never left Nevada had she not been continually plagued with illness and injury following a very serious bout of pneumonia with sepsis which had been further complicated by subsequent heart failure. Ruby had nearly been taken from Levi as a result. He'd been fairly young at the time and he'd been unable to really understand why Ruby's case had been so life-threatening, but it came on quickly and ravaged her body.

By the time Ruby had been released from the hospital she looked like an entirely different person. The experience had aged her and it was as if Ruby never completely recovered from it. The unfortunate side effect for Levi was becoming well acquainted with that sense of helplessness at a very young age. He couldn't lay all of that on the pneumonia; he'd gotten little tastes of it throughout his formative years due to his mother's infamously crazy lifestyle.

Nevertheless, none of that had prepared Levi for the terrifying vulnerability and sense of dread that followed him during the seven days that Ruby had lain in that hospital bed unable to catch her breath. She'd remained in isolation much of the time she spent in the hospital so he wasn't allowed to see her—couldn't sit by her bed or hold her hand.

Helpless.

Turning yet another corner, Levi navigated his way through the winding residential streets, pushing away all those memories which never failed to drag him down into darkness and fear. His foot pressed down on the accelerator and Levi took a deep breath, trying to hold back the anxiety that never completely went away—forever hovering there just underneath the surface of his skin.

Levi had allowed too much time to pass since he'd last checked in on Ruby. They'd talked on the phone, but his mother was notorious for randomly firing the nurses that Levi hired to care for her without informing him—which meant he was required to do random site visits. He tried distracting himself from the nagging fear that something was wrong by concentrating on the views all around him.

Driving past a few of the Tudor style bungalows, Levi smiled, recalling his fascination with that particular type when he was younger. Those homes had seemed the stuff of fairy tales to him as a child—Hansel and Gretel, Cinderella and all those dwarves who liked to follow Snow White around. He liked imagining those types of characters resided there, in Honeymoon Hills. He hadn't been an idiot child or anything, just had a tendency to try and escape reality whenever possible, because fantasy was oftentimes preferable to real life.

The instant Ruby had seen the photograph of the light pink, Streamline Moderne-style bungalow, she decided it belonged to her. She immediately fell in love with the Art Deco influenced architecture, though Levi suspected it had more to do with the pastel pink painted stucco than anything else.

The woman seriously loved the color pink.

Built in 1931, Ruby's bungalow was a rarity in Honeymoon Hills, constructed mainly of concrete and stucco, the curved corners and glass brick provided a sense of motion and all the filtered daylight made the interior feel light and airy. The low, horizontal, streamlined appearance and flat roof with no cornices or eaves made it stand out amongst all the others around it—much in the same way Ruby had always stood out in a crowd.

Turning onto Euclid Street, Levi frowned, seeing a squad car coming toward him from the opposite direction. A wave of nausea came over him, and he punched the gas as he maneuvered the car up the slight incline. His heart nearly stopped as he rounded the top of the small hill only to spot an ambulance parked in Ruby's driveway. He flung open the driver's side door before bringing the car to a tire-screeching halt on the street in front of Ruby's house. Cursing under his breath, Levi fumbled with the seat belt release which prevented him from exiting the car quickly enough.

Within seconds he was flying up the sidewalk that led to her front door which was standing wide open. He eyed the busted lock while sprinting through the front door, doing his best to keep the ever-growing panic boiling inside from taking him over completely. Levi stepped into the small foyer unsure what to do or where to go for a split second before racing past his old bedroom and poking his head into Ruby's to find no one was in there.

"Momma!" he called out, rushing back out to the foyer and past the dining room. It wasn't until he rounded the corner into the small kitchen that Levi spotted the paramedics standing in the living area at the back of the house.

His heart sank as the two men looked his direction.

"Mom?"

"She's okay, sir," one of the men said, making eye contact with him, further reassuring Levi that all was well. Or as well as they could be considering there was an ambulance parked outside the house.

Levi nodded, acknowledging he'd heard the man while scooching past him so he could get to Ruby.

She pulled the oxygen mask from her face and rolled her eyes. "I'm fine, darling, just had a dizzy spell."

She placed the mask back over her mouth and nose and took several deep breaths. Levi shut his eyes, trying to calm his nerves, only to feel Ruby grab his hand and give it a squeeze of reassurance.

He could hear the paramedics talking in low voices behind him and Levi struggled to listen as they discussed that the chief complaint was pain noted from the contusion in the temporal area of the skull from where Ruby had fallen and bumped her head on the floor.

"Are you bleeding anywhere?" Levi asked Ruby, who shook her head that she was not.

Levi went back to eavesdropping long enough to hear that her breathing had begun to normalize but her lungs sounded wheezy, bilaterally.

No big surprise there.

Her pulse was also strong, but seemed to be a little fast and her blood pressure was slightly elevated.

"But that is a normal reaction to the stress of all this, isn't it?" Levi asked, finally tearing his gaze away from his mother in order to turn around and face them.

The second EMT looked at Levi and for a moment, Levi thought he might be having a cardiac event all his own. The oddest sensation came over him, one he'd never experienced before and he immediately felt a light layer of sweat flush across the surface of his skin.

He smiled through the light-headed, slightly intoxicated feeling.

The paramedic eyed him somewhat suspiciously which registered that whatever was happening to Levi was evident to those around him. Since the EMT decided not to mention it, Levi saw no reason he shouldn't breeze right on past the tingles and mild case of nausea that continued to plague him.

"Hey...there, you." Levi smiled weakly while inappropriately staring into the bluest pair of eyes the world had no doubt ever known. They were arresting, those eyes—even the deepest, most crystal clear tropical waters of the Caribbean suffered in comparison.

Watching intently as the man came back around the coffee table and crouched down next to Ruby, Levi inventoried his dark, black hair and sexy stubble-covered masculine jawline which were softened by the warm smile as the man stared up at Levi from the floor where he knelt, attending to Ruby.

Levi felt it, like a fist in the gut.

"Say, you okay?" the guy asked. "You don't look so good."

"So-*whoa*-kay," Levi muttered, taking note that Ruby had also picked up on the fact something was up with her baby boy. "Though insulting me by noting my inadequate allure seems slightly uncalled for."

The guy's forehead crinkled up, visibly confused for a few moments before the dimples and perfect leading man smile spread across his face. "My apologies, sir. I wasn't referencing your physique so much as the slightly pained expression you were exhibiting."

Levi sat down on the other side of Ruby and did his level best to concentrate on the man's condescending tone as it irritated Levi and counteracted the dream-like spell he'd been under since laying eyes on him.

"What the hell happened here?" Levi began looking around for the nurse he was over-paying to watch after his mother. "And where the hell is Carrie?"

"Carrie?" Sexy, blue-eyes asked. "I'm Jake by the way… this is my partner, Craig."

"There was no one else here when we arrived on the scene," Craig said from behind him.

"Mom, where is your nurse?" He was staring at Jake again, but managed to tear his gaze away from the hypnotizing twin pools of mind-numbing sexiness long enough to turn his attention back to his mother. "She's supposed to have a nurse. I'm certainly still paying for a nurse."

Ruby plastered on her best, wide-eyed, innocent-of-any-wrong-doing expression and shrugged, clutching the mask to her mouth as if her very existence now depended upon each gulp of life-giving oxygen.

"You have got to stop firing the nurses I hire, Mom. Eventually we'll have run through all the nurses in the world and then where will we be?"

Ruby scowled, pulling the mask away. "This one prayed constantly, it was annoying and she refused to stop doing it when I asked her to."

Levi sighed, brushing a few strands of her platinum-dyed blonde hair off her forehead. He was trying to count to ten so he didn't come off like a monster-child by yelling at Ruby in front of complete strangers. He was also attempting to keep his focus on his mother and avoid getting lost in Paramedic Jake's dangerous Bermuda Triangle-like gaze once again.

"I asked nicely," Ruby muttered, "but she completely ignored me."

"I'm sure you did, Momma." Levi looked at Jake, but focused on his forehead. "Is she really all right?"

"She has a nasty bump on her head from where she fell and though she was conscious when we arrived on the scene, she was disoriented. She now appears to be lucid—

doesn't seem to have any trouble communicating, either." Jake winked at Ruby.

"Every time I said a curse word the woman would bow her head and pray," Ruby said, as if to further justify Nurse Carrie's dismissal.

Levi scowled at her. "She must have been praying a lot."

Jake and his partner both started chuckling when Ruby reached up and smacked Levi in the arm. He straightened out the hem of her floor length pink silk nightgown and tucked in the throw currently covering her legs.

"Momma, please, you're gonna have to start making some allowances for—"

"I shouldn't have to, not in my own home," she interrupted.

She started coughing and Levi sighed, already backing down, not wanting to send her into a coughing jag. She took his hand in hers, squeezing it—fully aware that was the closest to an apology he was going to get.

"How's my face, kiddo?" she asked, looking sweet and innocent once again.

Aside from the exhaustion, which was quite apparent, she looked no worse for the wear. She was made up from head to red-nail polished toe, thank goodness. Otherwise that would be all Ruby would be worried about. She was the vainest creature the world had ever known—Levi had the in-home hair care and mani-pedi bills to prove it.

"You look great, Mom." Levi turned to Jake. "Who called you?"

"A neighbor happened to be looking through the window there." Craig pointed to the window that looked out across the side yard into nosy Mrs. Miller's kitchen.

"Noticed your mother fall. Called 911 when they never saw Miss Ruby here get back up."

For the first time ever, Levi was grateful their busy-body neighbor had a penchant for peeping Tom-like behavior.

"Though we'd typically consider this a lift-assist as she seems alert and stable now, I am still recommending we get her to the hospital due to the contusion, let them run a CT scan and a few other tests—make sure everything checks out."

"That isn't necessary," Ruby said.

"They may want to keep her under observation overnight due to the head injury."

"I'm perfectly fine," she insisted.

"Thank you for that assessment, Mother, however, I think we'll follow the recommendations from the people with the actual medical training, just to be on the safe side."

"Does she have a history of respiratory issues?"

"She used to smoke like a fiend," he said accusingly, which garnered an eye roll from Ruby.

He barely got the entire spiel out, highlighting her pertinent medical history including that particularly nasty case of pneumonia, before Ruby cut him off.

"Killed my glorious career!"

"And we almost lost her," Levi said, shaking his head at her, still amazed that after all these years it was still all about her.

"Never fully recovered after," she added, completely ignoring Levi at this point.

Levi sighed, hoping to cut her off on the path to where she was no doubt heading. "She was a showgirl in Vegas back in the day."

"I was THE Vegas showgirl, damn it. I had legs for days and I knew how to use 'em. I set the city that never sleeps on fire throughout most of the eighties. It was fabulous. No one could touch me. I was fabulous."

She started coughing and Levi placed the oxygen mask back over her mouth. "She's a humble sorta gal."

"Lots of coke and loads of sex," Ruby said, pushing the oxygen mask away once again. "The music, the lights, the gorgeous, glittery costumes—"

"Which explains the tacky *I Dream of Jeannie* design scheme," Levi pointed around at the tone on tone pink paint and fabrics covered with lace and fringe.

"Don't interrupt your mother when she's reminiscing, child. I knew Sinatra, damn it."

He sighed, wondering why the hell she still thought knowing Sinatra back in the day meant she automatically garnered some sort of reverential respect.

"I'm guessing that when she said coke she wasn't referring to the refreshing beverage?" Jake asked, scribbling down notes into a wallet-sized booklet.

"Unfortunately, no." Levi strained his neck, trying to get a peek at what the man was writing. He glanced down at Ruby to see she wasn't real happy about Jake's documentation tactics either.

"Don't knock the cocaine, kiddo, you may not have ever been born without it."

Levi sighed. "And here we go."

"I'm… not going to ask." Jake pointed out, attempting to reassure Levi.

"Thank you," Levi said, trying not to smile back at the man.

"It was a fabulous orgy, Dr. Jake," Ruby said, ignoring Levi's plea and the fact Jake just stated he neither needed nor wanted any of the gory details.

Craig dramatically cleared his throat behind them, reminding Levi there were multiple witnesses to his humiliation. "The nice men don't want to hear about orgies, Momma," Levi pointed out, while gently petting her arm.

"I'm not a doctor, ma'am," Jake reminded her.

"You shouldn't be ashamed of where you come from," Ruby said, ignoring Jake's disclaimer while shooing Levi's hand away. "It's not a very becoming quality in a man."

"Forgive me, Mother, I'll be sure to bring that up at my next children-of-orgies support group meeting."

Ruby rolled her eyes. "So sarcastic this one—it's no wonder you're still single."

"You musta been one helluva party girl," Jake said, smiling at her without any sort of discernible judgment on his face.

Just like that he'd managed to snake charm Ruby, who had forgotten all about Levi's smart mouth. It was one of the single sexiest things Levi had ever witnessed and made him feel better that Ruby seemed to also be susceptible to Jake's super-human charms.

A little hinky, perhaps, considering they were parent and child, but sometimes strange company was better than no company at all.

It was a special brand of man who wasn't put off by Ruby's brazenness. Her behavior tended to work as a litmus test for most mortals—often revealing the ugly, pretentious side most people attempted to conceal from people they were trying to impress. Even the guys who liked to crystal up and fuck their brains out every weekend could be a little judgey when it came to Ruby's tales of drunken debauchery. Totally hypocritical, mind you, though Levi wasn't into that type of guy anyway, and truth be told, he was usually way more embarrassed by his mother than anyone else ever had been, so he tried not to pass judgment when he could help it.

Parental introductions had been the thing he'd passionately avoided for as long as possible when dating a new guy—back when he actually had time to date. Levi had lost more than one man due to his mother over the years, but on some level, he had self-justified those experiences in her favor. Any guy who would leave him because his mother was a total crackpot was likely not the kind that would end up sticking around long-term regardless.

In that sense, she had done him a solid.

He and Ruby were polar opposites—Ruby had no filter and Levi was nothing but filter.

Levi was a lot like the parties he planned, on the exterior all seemed calm, collected and always appeared to be completely under control. Each event was like an opera, a production for the masses who never witnessed the inevitable chaos—the by-product of all the moving parts running behind the scenes. Levi was the great and powerful Oz and he liked keeping all his shit tucked safely behind the curtain. Needless to say, that often included Ruby.

It didn't mean he didn't love her. There had been times when he was younger when he'd allowed his resentment of Ruby and his completely insane upbringing to cast a cloud over their relationship. But the older he got the more protective he became, and Levi had developed some semblance of respect and genuine admiration for her. Much like her name, Ruby was unique and precious, a rare jewel. Levi didn't necessarily enjoy putting his Ruby on display all the time, yet he was also terrified of losing her.

Attempting to take care of her was frustrating as she was more than a handful. You couldn't make her do anything she didn't want to do. Their relationship had become Levi attempting to find ways to work around her wants, in order to ensure he managed to meet all her needs.

All that glitters isn't gold.

"For the record, I like a guy with a smart mouth." Jake smiled at Levi before glancing back at Ruby.

Ruby was grinning and Levi realized he was as well, something his mother unfortunately took note of.

"I'll go grab the gurney." Craig thumbed toward the front of the house and Jake nodded. He grabbed the handheld radio on his collar and began speaking to whoever was on the other end as he left the room.

Levi was too distracted by Jake to pay attention to what Craig was saying.

There was something about him—Jake seemed familiar to Levi in some odd way. There was a genuineness that came off the man in waves, like he was completely comfortable in his own skin—allowing him the luxury of accepting everyone else for who they were. It was as if Jake had this blanketed, face-value respect for those who were different than he was, like each individual made up a new thread that wove itself into the tapestry of Jake's life, enriching and strengthening him from within.

Levi shook loose all the romantic nonsense that was bouncing around inside his head, reminding himself to get a fucking grip already. The man was fucking gorgeous and all, but the delusions of grandeur were a little much and very un-Levi-like.

One thing was certain, Jake appeared to be sincerely interested in and amused by anything Ruby had to say. Unfortunately, Ruby had also picked up on that fact.

"That's how my Levi got his name, remember, sweetie?" Ruby smiled up at him, forever ignorant to the fact Levi didn't find his orgy-origin-story the least bit charming. "I never caught his father's name, but I do recall he was a beautiful hunk of man… wore the tightest pair of hip and ass hugging Levis I'd ever seen on a man."

Levi groaned, desperately wishing she would stop already. "Feel free to give her a sedative if you think it appropriate."

"Like they were painted on, those jeans," Ruby added, staring off in space.

Jake laughed while continually checking her vitals.

"Your daddy had the most beautiful thighs I've ever seen on any man, I do remember that much."

"Dear God," Levi muttered.

Jake stood, placing a hand on Levi's shoulder, appearing to be amused by it all. "If it makes you feel any better, I can't say the same about my father."

The squeeze of reassurance he gave went straight to Levi's crotch and he had to fight to maintain any sort of composure. He managed to forget about his mother for several moments while staring up at the paramedic, admiring the way his hair was styled—neatly parted to the side and sleekly combed over like he'd walked off of the set of *Mad Men*. His stubble was well-groomed so Levi could tell it was intentional and not due to the fact he'd neglected to shave the last few days. He also had totally suckable, thick, light-pink lips that practically called out to Levi, as if begging to be kissed.

A man like that he'd be willing… hell, eager to make time for… busy schedule be damned. And that was merely Levi's reaction from the neck up.

"Hey, she's going to be all right," Jake squeezed his shoulder again.

He immediately felt like a shit-heel considering Jake had mistaken Levi's lusting over him for concern over his mother's well-being.

"Thanks." Levi forced a smile.

He gave Levi another pat, before Jake's hand slid down to his bicep, offering Levi two more quick squeezes before awkwardly pulling his hand away.

"Apologies for the inappropriate… fondling there." He shook his head like he might be confused by his own behavior.

"I don't mind." Levi felt his eyes widening, realizing the way that sounded. "The inappropriate fondling… I didn't take it that way, is what I meant to say there."

Jake laughed, glancing down at Ruby, making Levi fear he'd embarrassed Jake.

"I see crackles," Ruby said, looking back and forth between the two of them.

"Crackles?" Jake looked confused, likely thinking she was experiencing issues with her vision.

"For the record, my son is single." Ruby smiled sweetly at Jake, avoiding any eye contact with Levi. "He goes down to the Cinema Paradise every Thursday night for their Classic Film festival. You should meet him there."

Jake grinned, winking at her as he began to put the pieces together.

"Mother, please," Levi pleaded. "I'm sure Jake has better things to do with his time."

"I like movies," Jake said, nodding.

"Yeah, sure, but you don't have to, I mean, she'll be heavily medicated at some point, and won't remember this anyway."

"I heard that," Ruby muttered, sounding calmer. "Sparks are rare, baby boy. You should never ignore the crackles."

Jake grinned, flashing those pearly whites. "What movie is playing this week?"

Levi felt his face flush with heat once again and found it momentarily difficult to swallow. "Some Like It… Hot."

"I've heard some people do," Jake said.

Levi couldn't tell for sure whether Jake was actually flirting or if he was merely attempting to help Levi out by giving him props in front of Ruby. Obviously, the whole flirting scenario was preferable, but either way Levi considered it a kindness, though the latter made him feel slightly losery.

"I don't think I have any plans this Thursday, assuming you wouldn't mind the company?" Jake asked.

Levi had to fight hard in order to maintain control over himself, but he did a celebratory, mental fist-pump.

"No, that's… seven o'clock… that's when it starts… the movie, I mean," Levi said, tripping over his own words.

Please stop speaking freak-a-zoid.

"That's good," Ruby muttered, grinning at the two of them, visibly pleased with herself. "My Levi needs more friends, I worry he won't have enough people to take care of him."

"She's quite a character." Jake smirked as Ruby pretended like she'd stopped listening. "And very sweet."

"For an ex-gangster's-gun-moll slash Vegas showgirl, yeah… she's kinda sweet… in her own way."

Jake took a few steps back, signaling for Levi to follow. "She was pretty frightened and confused before you showed up."

Levi nodded, looking down at her and feeling terrible that he hadn't been there for her.

"I think all is clear, but getting her to the hospital for some tests will confirm we didn't miss anything. My real concern is whether she fell or fainted."

"Okay, sure, though she does suffer occasional bouts of vertigo, which is why we have the nurse in the first place."

"She goes through a lot of them, huh?" Jake asked.

"Unfortunately, yes." Levi glanced down, catching her doing a horrible job pretending not to eavesdrop. "She can be a handful."

Jake scribbled something else down in his tiny notebook.

Craig called out for help with the gurney from somewhere at the front of the house and Jake ran off.

Levi watched her for a moment as she stared up at the ceiling of her living room. He could tell she was anxious. She'd had a not-so-unnatural fear of hospitals since nearly dying in one all those years ago. In all fairness, Levi didn't particularly have the warm-n-fuzzies for them either, and she'd landed back in the hospital many times over the years due to bronchial issues which continued to plague her.

Ruby was terrified she'd go into the hospital one of these times and never come back out. He had that same fear, but kept it to himself.

In the time it took them to get Ruby onto the gurney and loaded into the ambulance Levi called his handyman to come out and fix the front door. He gave Jake his cell phone number and asked him to call in the event there were any complications. He hated not getting into the back of that ambulance with her, but he wanted to stay behind and make sure they secured the house before he left.

As the ambulance pulled away, he made a second call to inquire about finding Ruby yet another nurse. He was a little relieved to get the voicemail of the home health service as they were well acquainted with both Levi and Ruby. To say her reputation preceded her was an understatement, but he was also pretty irritated no one had called to inform him that Ruby had let the previous nurse go. That was bullshit and he'd have plenty to say about it. Levi was aware he was upset and a little emotional, neither of which were likely to aid him during the confrontation that was coming.

He stood on the front porch, shivering as the sun was beginning to set, allowing a slight chill in the air to set in. All he could do now was wait—one of his least favorite things. That familiar sense of helplessness came over him and Levi fought hard to force it down.

There wasn't time for irrational fear now.

He needed to be the rock that his Ruby could cling to until this storm finally passed. He turned and went back inside the house, pushing the door closed behind him, deciding to keep himself occupied by straightening up while he waited.

Distraction over distress had always gotten him through the tough times and today would be no different.

CHAPTER THREE

Levi was aware that he was being silly—waiting outside the box office of the Cinema Paradise at Main and Elm for a guy he was fairly certain wouldn't show up. Watching a brown leaf scraping along the sidewalk as the wind forced it into movement, he laughed to himself, thinking it was a fairly accurate representation of his love life. Pinning all his hopes on Jake the paramedic to resuscitate his lonely heart was likely asking too much for one man, but Levi couldn't seem to help himself.

He stood, huddled under the huge marquee which jutted off the building and looked like the grill of a classic car—gentle curves and distinct lines emblazoned in red and gold neon. It was an impressive feature that covered half the sidewalk. The Arabian Nights, Moroccan-themed architectural style was stunning both inside and out. The theatre itself was every bit the escape into a fantasy land as the movies that were projected upon the big screen.

Levi glanced through the glass into the lobby taking in the deep red and gold carpet and the elaborate gold-gilded concession stand. Moviegoers had paid ten cents back when the Cinema Paradise first opened its doors in 1924. The theatre had undergone an extensive restoration back in the early nineties, and the end result had given new life to a beautiful and unique part of Wilde City's history.

Glancing at his watch yet again, Levi realized his nerves were making it difficult to distract himself. In the three days since Levi had first encountered Jake, he had a terrible time trying to focus on much else. The fact he hadn't heard from Jake the paramedic, despite having given the man his cell number during all the Ruby-drama, had Levi leaning toward the conclusion that any connection he'd detected between the two them had been completely imagined.

Yet here he stood, pacing back and forth out in the cold air, reeking of desperation.

"So unattractive," he muttered to himself before blowing warm air onto his hands while wishing he'd had the forethought to grab the pair of gloves from his car.

All negativity aside, part of him was hoping that he was wrong and Jake would show up after all. One-sided or not, Levi had never felt anything like this for an otherwise perfect stranger. There had been an instant connection on his end and he was anxious to find out if it would still be there now, or had it already run its course. It seemed inconceivable either way he looked at it. Now that his professional career was finally beginning to take off, it wouldn't suck to have a… someone.

He wasn't a greedy man, Levi just wanted *the one*, someone—and not like Ruby who'd had more 'ones' than he could count using all his fingers and toes combined. Truth be told, none of Ruby's men had ever treated him poorly, but he'd gotten so used to having men come in and out of his life as a child that he wondered if that hadn't scarred him in some unseen way. In spite of wanting to find 'the one' he feared deep down that once found, his 'one' would end up leaving him the way all of Ruby's had abandoned her.

He cringed at that thought, glancing around at the people passing him by on their way inside the theatre, wondering if they knew he was getting stood up.

"Very cold hands," he muttered, shoving them into his jeans pockets.

He was aware it was silly, not walking the half a block back to his car to grab the damn gloves but he couldn't seem to force himself to leave, fearing Jake would show up and think Levi hadn't bothered to come.

His extremities had begun to go numb due to the twenty degree drop in the temperature that happened throughout the day and he cursed cold-fronts in general, declaring them an agent of the devil and a sure sign of the impending apocalypse.

Stupid Beelzebub and his rotten shenanigans, no wonder the fucker had been banished to hell.

Frostbite was no laughing matter considering Levi had grown attached to all his bits and baubles. He stopped pacing for a moment, remembering that movie about the rugby team that crashed in the snowy mountains and were forced to eat their dead teammates in order to survive. He was pretty sure he wouldn't have it in him to do that— *maybe*—if it were like people he didn't know, he could perhaps eat them in that situation. But how do you go home after getting rescued and explain to their very confused loved ones exactly what happened to your dead teammate's right butt cheek?

Apologies, but we got a bit peckish up there and baby had back, m'kay?

Awkward doesn't even begin to cover that conversation. Butt cheeks don't typically wander off on their own, right? He looked around, expecting to get an amen or something, then shook the ever-encroaching insanity from his head.

"Can't for the life of me imagine why someone hasn't snatched me up yet," he said under his breath. "Keep your crazy to yourself, cracker."

His ass bleeped so he reluctantly reached into his back pocket and pulled out his phone. Valerie had sent him a text with an attachment, which was never a good sign. Levi tapped the screen, opening the photo that came with the disclaimer:

Hope your mystery date is doing this to you.

A .gif popped up of two guys fucking doggy style. They'd sped the frame up so much that it looked more like a perverted Looney Tunes cartoon than anything intended to actually arouse.

He turned off the phone altogether wondering why he put up with her nonsense. He decided to give Jake five more minutes before throwing in the towel and going in alone. It then occurred to him to stop being so hard on Valerie. How rude, really, all she wanted to do was get him laid. He wasn't exactly a saint, by any means—though lately it just hadn't seemed worth the effort.

The sensation of being watched came over Levi and when turning to his right, he spotted the lady sitting inside the ticket booth who was staring at him. Her pity-expression was unmistakable. She knew he was getting stood up, too. It was humiliating enough that she'd asked him to verify three times that he wanted to purchase *two* tickets for the movie this week.

So yeah, he typically came to the movies by himself.

Was it necessary to act as if the world had spun off its axis at the thought he might actually have a real date?

The thing that he'd never understood to begin with was why people got so hinky about going to the movies alone? He'd have never thought anything of it if other people hadn't made such a big deal about it. Valerie acted as if going alone to a movie theatre was worse than catching an STD. Why anyone required a companion to go sit in a darkened theatre, where conversation was typically frowned upon, was beyond him. Add to that fact, when watching a movie, people were supposed to be looking up at the screen, not at the person sitting next to them, so Levi was at a loss over the whole thing.

Levi's eyes bugged out slightly, seeing the ticket booth lady grinning at him like a total freak. Then she started pointing at him and he began to get pissed, thinking she was now making fun of him for getting stood up.

Totally f'in rude!

He screamed and nearly jumped out of his skin when someone grabbed his shoulder and said, "Hello."

Levi's reaction had in turn scared the crap out of Jake, who had taken a few steps back while clasping his hand over his heart as if attempting to keep it from popping out of his chest.

"Shit, dude," Jake said, starting to chuckle.

"Sorry… so… *gah*… sorry." Levi reached over, briefly taking Jake's hand to punctuate his apology with a gentle squeeze.

"Think we should take our act on the road?" Jake asked, nudging his head to Levi's side.

He turned to see the ticket booth bitch was laughing her ass off at the two of them, all but hunched over as she wiped her eyes which had apparently teared up in amusement. She was shaking her hand at them as if that was supposed to suffice as some sort of an apology.

It was at that point Levi started to laugh as well.

Jake shook his head. "Let me go grab a ticket, so we can get out of this cold."

He looked every bit as dreamy as Levi remembered, potentially even more so considering three days absence had definitely made his heart grow fonder.

He fished his wallet from his back pocket and pulled out two tickets. "I've got you covered."

Jake's eyebrows arched, signifying he was surprised by that. "You were pretty confident I was coming then?"

"You're welcome." Levi grinned, handing Jake one of the tickets while adding sarcastically, "Most men find me irresistible, so you showing up is not so much of a shock."

Jake pulled open one of the massive glass and brass doors, insisting Levi go in first. "I see, and I thank you for the ticket and insist on purchasing the popcorn and beverages."

"You have yourself a deal, mister," Levi said.

"Had for the price of movie theatre snacks?" Jake hissed. "I'm disappointed, Levi. I'd planned on having to work *much* harder to impress you."

"I'm a concession stand slut from way back," Levi said, sniffing and puffing himself up while pulling up on his britches.

Jake laughed, taking Levi by the arm and leading him through the lobby and into one of the lines at the concession stand.

Walking through the doors into theatre was like being enveloped in opulence. The wood beams and ornate detail throughout the interior were actually molded plaster which had been painstakingly refurbished during the remodel. Levi imagined what it must have been like for the average-Joe back in the day, before the internet and ease of travel had been developed.

Must've been like walking into another world.

"You didn't have to wait outside for me in the cold, FYI," Jake said as they waited patiently for the people in front of them to decide what snacks to get. "I could have found you inside."

"I was afraid you wouldn't be able to find me without a little help considering I wasn't unconscious or flailing about on the ground bleeding out."

"Very funny."

"What? Like I'm supposed to trust the skills of a man who never has to go out searching for things because his employer tells him where to find the bodies all day long?"

"For the record," Jake gave him the stink-eye, insinuating he might not be appreciating the smart-assery, "collecting bodies sounds more like something the morgue would handle. EMTs are typically sent out in search of people who need our lifesaving skills."

"Nice… I like the way you slipped that whole lifesaving, I'm-a-hero bit in there, very smooth."

"Thank you, thank you very much." Jake followed that up with a quick wink, reassuring Levi that he did indeed appreciate the attempt at banter.

They decided to share a large bag of popcorn, sans extra butter, and each got their own soda. The gal behind the counter seemed unamused by Levi's winsome tale about the fact he and Jake were new friends and thus not ready for the drink sharing stage of their relationship.

Jake was mortified, planting his face firmly into the palm of his hand, which oddly enough, Levi found endearing.

By the time they made their way into the theatre and found decent seats toward the back of the auditorium the opening credits were already running. A night time sky complete with twinkling stars and floating clouds hung over the Arabian courtyard themed auditorium. It seemed magical to Levi, and had always been his favorite part of the theatre.

"It's pretty," Jake whispered, pointing up at the ceiling.

Levi smiled and nodded while placing his drink into the cup holder on his right. He scooched far enough back into the seat so the bag of popcorn would fit wedged between his legs.

"I can hold the popcorn if you want," Jake whispered.

"Nice try, buddy," Levi said with a smirk.

"What?" he asked, cringing when the couple sitting in front of them each turned and gave them a stern, withering glare. "It's the friggin' opening credits, people!"

They turned back around but seemed unfazed by Jake's credits clarification.

"I only offered in an attempt to be chivalrous," Jake continued, motioning toward the popcorn.

"I'm no dummy, fresh off the farm, pal. The one who has the corn, holds all the power."

Jake started snickering over that, covering his mouth with his hand until he managed to maintain control over himself once again.

"That is easily one of the silliest things I've ever heard," he said, cocking his head to the side as if to punctuate the seriousness of his disclaimer.

"Spoken like someone who isn't holding the corn," Levi said, smiling evilly.

As if to further prove he had no desire to hold the popcorn Jake reached over and calmly grabbed a handful and began eating it. "Tastes good to me."

Levi started laughing which had Jake grinning until he noticed the cranky couple had turned around once again.

"Movie's that way." Jake pointed for them to turn back around and mind their own business.

"So disruptive," Levi whispered, shaking his head at Jake as if it were all his fault.

Jake pointed toward the screen for Levi to pay attention to the movie as well.

* * * *

About thirty minutes into the movie, which Levi had barely been able to follow despite having seen this particular film on multiple occasions, he began to take note of a particularly odd sensation taking place between his legs each time Jake reached into the bag of popcorn. About three-fourths of the buttery snack was now gone so when Jake shoved his hand down there, fingers rummaging around to grab a handful of buttery, crunchy goodness, Levi was inadvertently receiving a complimentary nads-massage.

It was more than a little disconcerting considering he always got popcorn when he came to the movies and he always placed the bag in the exact same location where the current one now resided. Apparently he'd fondled his own nuts for so many years now that he no longer took notice when he came to the theatre by himself and was rummaging around the bottom of the bag.

That was mildly disturbing but he tried not to take it personally that his own balls were pretty much over him.

Talk about the ultimate snub.

He watched as Jake's hand reached over and back down. He didn't move a muscle though he could feel his cock swelling with each swish of Jake's hand in the bottom of the bag.

Christ, is he digging for gold down there or what?

He turned to look at Jake, who seemed to be taking his sweet time as he rooted around for the perfect handful of corn. It was obvious he wasn't paying any attention to what he was doing but at some point he seemed to realize Levi was staring at him so he turned and smiled for a moment. He glanced down at his hand which was shoved between Levi's legs and his smile faded slightly when he realized what was happening.

Jake ripped his hand out of the bag so fast several pieces of popcorn came flying out with it, shooting up into the air like confetti, which sprinkled down upon the two of them as well as several strangers sitting around them.

Naturally the glaring couple in front of them ended up getting pelted with several pieces, which didn't go over so well as the man sat all the way up in his seat like he was getting ready to make each of them a knuckle sandwich.

"Sorry!" Levi whispered. "There was a spider... I panicked... my hand twitched... popcorn went flying... totally my bad."

The lady shot out of her seat and began swatting at her arms and shoulders.

"Dead... spider dead... totally killed that fucker," Levi said, attempting to reassure the arachnophobic woman he'd unintentionally terrified with his off-the-cuff lie intended to cover up the unintentional ball-fluffing that still had him semi-erect.

The lady sat back down and everyone sitting around them finally settled back down and went back to watching the movie.

Several minutes went by before Levi, who was totally humiliated, finally dared to look over at Jake—whose entire body was shaking from laughter. His hand was planted firmly over his mouth, stifling any noise, but his eyes were watering so much it looked like he might be crying.

Jake pulled his hand away long enough to mouth the words, *I'm so sorry*, before having to cover up again, unable to maintain control over himself.

Levi was a little annoyed, mostly because he was still aroused with no assurances that there was any relief coming his way anytime soon. More than anything he was embarrassed, and thus felt the need to clarify so he leaned over, whispering into Jake's ear.

"Didn't really consider the logistics of the popcorn placement ahead of time."

Jake eyed him suspiciously. "So you didn't place it there on purpose? Hoping for a little incidental gropage?"

"No!"

Shushing once again came from several people around them but the angry dude sitting in front of them didn't even bother turning around this time, settling for shaking his head in disapproval while keeping his eyes facing forward.

Jake bit down on his lip to keep himself from breaking out in laughter again. Once he settled back down he leaned over and whispered, "Wow, defensive much? Sounded a little haughty there, if you ask me."

Levi whispered back. "I didn't ask."

"So you're a totally clueless, accidentally pervy prick tease?"

Levi's mouth fell open and he was grateful for the darkness of the theatre which masked the redness of his flushed cheeks.

"That might actually make you even more attractive—which is saying something 'cause you're pretty damn cute to start with."

Levi smiled, shaking his head slightly while resisting the overwhelming urge to lean over and kiss the man. "You're a lot prettier when you're not talking."

Jake chuckled, doing his best to not make a further spectacle.

God, how he wanted to kiss Jake. He couldn't manage to follow what was happening between Marilyn and Tony Curtis on-screen because all he could think about was leaning over and kissing Jake-the-paramedic off-screen.

That urge to lock lips was so strong that the not-doing-of-it was very likely every bit as titillating as the act itself would no doubt be.

Christ, I'm still half-hard. This is bad—really bad!

It couldn't possibly be good to like a guy this much before knowing anything about him.

Danger… danger, Will Robinson!

Levi grinned, forcing his attention back on Marilyn. Sad. So sad, she seemed. Beautiful, but sad. Just behind her eyes there was a loneliness that Levi recognized.

Also a totally underrated actress…

He inhaled sharply, but quickly recovered, holding his breath as his gaze landed on the armrest sitting between him and Jake.

Our hands are totally touching!

And he was apparently a twelve-year-old girl trapped inside the body of a thirty-one-year-old gay man. He rolled his eyes, chastising himself.

The theatre erupted in laughter and Levi joined in, though he was doing so more from the sensation of giddiness that had filled his chest from the physical contact. For the first time in a very long time there was a tiny kernel of hope burning deep inside his chest that maybe... *just maybe...* something real was finally happening for him.

Jake turned to look at him and Levi met his gaze. They each grinned before turning their attention back to the screen, laughing again as Jack Lemmon batted his eyelashes.

He watched Jake glance down at their hands as well. His fingers brushed gently over Levi's hand before he pulled his away, folding his arms across his chest and turning his attention back to the screen.

Levi awkwardly removed his limb from the arm rest, placing the bag of popcorn on the floor. That finger graze was quite possibly the most erotic thing that happened to him in a good year. That fact was more than a little depressing, but he'd long ago accepted the fact that he was the type who would rather be alone and celibate as opposed to settling for anything less than full-on, crazy-in-love romance. If Levi didn't feel it and if he didn't believe the object of his affection did as well, he didn't waste his time or energy.

In his thirty-one years, he'd never felt anything like this—slightly manic, difficult to concentrate on anything else sort of chest-achy fear and hope all tangled up and intertwined...threatening happiness or heartbreak...or potentially both just over the horizon.

* * * *

Standing awkwardly on the sidewalk outside the theatre as the last of the other moviegoers finished filing out of the brass and glass doors, Levi and Jake stood there face to face, not saying a word, just staring into one another's eyes. The occasional car whizzed by them and Levi could hear and see other people out of the corner of his eye, saying goodbyes to friends or walking hand-in-hand toward their cars or homes or perhaps making their way out for cocktails and eventually, totally inappropriate sex with one another, if they were lucky.

It all sounded like a recipe for success to Levi at the moment.

Kiss me, for God's sake man, please fucking kiss me.

He'd been saying that over and over inside his own head like a mantra, as if thinking it enough times might actually will it into reality.

"I had fun," Jake said, his gorgeous eyes seemingly forever focused on Levi's lips.

"Me too," Levi said, unable to make himself stop chewing on his lower lip while taking a step closer, hoping that would be enough of a signal for Jake to bring on the wet, hot, mouth-to-mouth he'd no doubt offered countless other strangers in an attempt to save lives over the years. It certainly felt as if Levi's life hung in the freakin' balance, so why wasn't Paramedic Jake saving him?

Jake's lips curled slightly, a clue Levi took to mean he had noticed the cue.

It was times like this that Levi wished he were a more aggressive and forward kinda guy—the type who wouldn't stand there waiting to be kissed like some stereotypical 1950s Annette Funicello archetype. He blamed his mother for this particular personality flaw. No one had ever accused Ruby of being demure—though there had been several who had suggested she might try to be, over the years.

Levi never wanted to be like that, forever afraid of mixing up all the signals and forcing himself upon some poor sap who didn't share the same feelings.

It was a crippling fear for Levi.

"Maybe we could do this again sometime?" Jake asked, clearing his throat.

Levi nodded, inadvertently taking yet another tiny step closer as he tried to flush all the negativity from his entirely too-neurotic brain. "I'd like that, Jake."

They each smiled and Jake finally started to lean in.

Levi pretty much stopped breathing in that moment, his vision getting hazy as Jake got closer. He could feel Jake's breath brushing across his face when something wet smacked him hard in the forehead.

Jake leaned back, wiping water off his face that had splattered there, ricocheting off Levi.

"What the hell?" Levi wiped his forehead, looking at Jake who had started laughing. "Was that a raindrop?"

"I'm pained at the thought it might be anything else," Jake said, his voice laced with amusement.

Levi frowned as a mental list including bird shit, urine and a multitude of other unseemly possibilities occurred to him.

Seconds later the dark skies overhead opened up and it began to pour. Large raindrops that almost stung when striking the skin; both men were completely drenched in the seconds it took them to find cover under the theatre marquee.

"Wow," Jake said, trying to shake the water off his jacket as he stared out across the street, dumbfounded.

"That's freakin' crazy," Levi said, his teeth already beginning to chatter thanks to unforgiving combination of cold air and wet clothes.

"Guess we should probably—"

"Right, sure, that's probably a good idea," Levi said, cutting Jake off while cursing the cruel universe for interrupting what would have no doubt been an epic friggin' kiss.

They were each shivering and cold and the mood was most definitely ruined—a fact that didn't manage to deter random thoughts that included inviting Jake back to his loft for a desperately needed bout of power-fucking. Not typically Levi's style, though that didn't appear to be pertinent in that precise moment, even though sex with guys he didn't know had never really gone well for him.

"I'm this way," Jake said, thumbing the opposite direction from where Levi was parked. "You?"

Levi pointed the other direction and Jake sort of chuckled and Levi tried to not imagine that it was relief he was seeing on Jake's face.

"I've got your cell," Jake said, nodding.

"Right." Levi crossed his arms, dreading the mad dash through the rain to get to his car while also desperate to get anywhere that might be warm. "Thanks for checking on Ruby yesterday. She told me you stopped by to see her before they released her from the hospital."

"No problem, was my pleasure," Jake said through chattering teeth. "Miss Ruby is pretty awesome."

Without thinking Levi tossed his arms around Jake, giving him a good squeeze and a peck on the cheek. Jake hugged him back, albeit it a little awkwardly, so Levi let him go and took off running without making eye contact.

He wasn't sure why or how, but whatever heat had been there moments before when they'd nearly kissed had evaporated in an instant. He was hoping it was just the colder-than-cuss rain, but if that wasn't the case, Levi didn't want to ruin the fantasy playing out in his own mind by bearing witness to any sort of change on Jake's face.

By the time he made it to his car he glanced back down the street toward the theatre. Jake was no longer there. Levi fired up the engine, adjusting the vents while waiting for the car to warm up.

Through vigorously chattering teeth, he said a little prayer that tonight wouldn't be all there was between he and Jake, while doing his best to temper any expectations he had about Jake-the-paramedic.

"And seriously, dude, if there is a next time, try expending a little extra effort and find out the man's last name before attempting to accept parts of his anatomy into your body."

He glanced up at his reflection in the rear view mirror.

"Tacky ho."

CHAPTER FOUR

Julia Freeman-Kingsley's penthouse was located on the eighteenth floor of what had originally been the Wilkes Regency Hotel, built in 1924. Newspaper tycoon and entrepreneur, Thaddeus Wilkes married socialite, Louella Landerson and subsequently commissioned the beaux-arts high-rise. The penthouse had been designed specifically to house Wilkes and his new bride; however Thaddeus died under mysterious circumstances before construction was completed.

At the time it was rumored to have been a mob hit, retribution for Thaddeus's brutal assault on the ever growing criminal element taking over the city. Wilkes had made a great many enemies as he'd continually splashed scathing indictments across the front pages of the Wilde City Gazette for months at a time—refusing to let up on those responsible for attempting to bring about the ruination of 'his' city.

Now considered a historical landmark, the building had been repurposed as condominiums back in the late '90s. Constructed out of concrete, limestone and brick, the exterior had been meticulously restored. Much of the interior had been gutted during the remodel, however nearly all of the original architecture and interior finishes of the penthouse and the restaurant called Louella's, located on the main floor, had been preserved.

Levi felt like a total history geek in that precise moment, standing awkwardly in the massive living room waiting for the mistress of the house to show her face. He'd gone a little manic back when he was researching the city in preparation for the planning of and subsequent bidding for the Cancer Benefit. He'd continued to do research on the history of the city whenever time allowed, deciding it gave him an edge.

Knowledge is supposedly power after all.

The penthouse itself was over seven thousand square feet with an additional two thousand in outdoor space which included a solarium and two terraces—all featuring spectacular views of the water on one side, and the cityscape from the other.

"The annual property taxes must be a real bitch," he muttered, re-reminding himself not to touch anything, considering everything in the place likely cost more than he would ever be worth.

Levi had heard rumors that the penthouse had been a combined wedding present to Julia and Gregory, paid for by both sets of the parents—probably the reason why rich people liked marrying other rich people so much. These families were in that class of individuals who concerned themselves with creating dynasties, and shit. While Levi certainly wanted to be comfortable, he had no desire to be this kind of wealthy, fairly certain he wouldn't know what to do with himself if he were.

Julia's assistant, Jane Meadows, poked her head around the corner. "She'll be right with you, Mr. Goode."

Her dark red hair was pulled back into a meticulously groomed bun and her black framed, cat-eye glasses sat pertly atop the bridge of her nose. Levi was a bit surprised Julia's personal assistant was so attractive, though it spoke volumes about the confidence Julia had in her marriage.

"Please, call me Levi," he said, figuring Julia operated on a more familiar first-name basis remembering that she insisted Levi call her by her first name combined with the new intel that her PA also referred to her as Julia.

"Can I get you anything while you wait?" she asked, smiling pleasantly.

"No, thank you for offering, though."

"Alrighty," she said, spinning on her heel and disappearing back down the hall.

The sound of her bare feet padding against the hard woods momentarily distracted him. It was totally weird, he thought, glancing down at his argyle-socked feet, wiggling his toes and trying to ignore the fact he felt completely naked being shoeless in such a fancy environment. He'd thought the gal who answered the front door had been joking when she asked him to remove them until he noticed the elaborate shelving built specifically to house the footwear of visitors such as himself.

Germaphoba-freaky.

"It's completely ludicrous, I know," Julia said, breezing into the room looking cool as a cucumber wearing pale grey, tailored slacks and a flowy cream silk blouse. "I have a thing about outside dirt getting tracked in—my apologies."

Levi shrugged, laughing awkwardly. "Su casa es mi...do whatever the hell you want."

Julia motioned for him sit. "Can I get you anything to drink?"

"I've got a bottle of water in my bag, but thank you."

"Okay then." Julia took a seat on the sofa across from him as Levi sat down in the cream-colored silk upholstered chair. "My parents will be here any minute. I'd hoped to have a little more time to prep you—give you some pointers and what-not—it's really great seeing you again, by the way."

"Thank you, I've been looking forward to seeing you as well." Levi crossed his legs and leaned back in the chair. "That being said, you can totally relax, I've got this, Julia. I've done my homework."

"They will try backing you into a corner, making you think they have zero intentions of hiring you in an attempt to force you into a rate reduction."

"That wouldn't shock me one bit."

"Don't you dare do it, Levi, I'll be very angry if you do."

That took him by surprise.

She rolled her eyes while nodding slightly. "That wasn't meant to be a rich girl bragging about the fact she has money, by the way."

"I never thought that," Levi insisted, which seemed to put her at ease.

"I think you're worth every penny you charge—whatever that happens to be—and I don't want you taking any sort of a pay cut just so Daddy can feel like he's a big man in control of the entire universe."

"That's quite possibly one of the nicest things anyone has ever said about me."

"What?" she asked, appearing completely horrified. "That's the saddest thing I've ever heard, Levi Goode. I'm going to take you under my wing, young man. You're sorely in need of better friends if that is the best compliment you've ever had."

Levi could feel the heat flushing his cheeks, but he was happy that his initial impressions of her were reaffirmed in that moment. "I would no doubt be quite lucky to count you as a friend, Julia."

"Lovely, that's all settled then!" She appeared genuinely pleased.

He wondered if perhaps she might be sorely in need of friends herself, imagining that a great many people might envy her to the extent she couldn't ever allow her guard to drop completely.

"There's something different about you?" Julia asked, looking him over suspiciously.

"Don't think so," he said.

"You look kind of…glowy." She nodded as if reconfirming for herself that she was on the right track.

Levi worried for a moment that he might be nervous sweating, and then he forced a grin, wondering if she meant—

"That's it, right there." Julia nodded, knowingly. "You met someone."

He shrugged. "Maybe, we'll see."

"You're blushing!" Julia began giggling. "You really like him."

"Perhaps."

"Who is he and how did you meet?" she asked, clapping giddily. "Tell me everything."

He didn't say anything at first. The last thing Levi wanted her to know was he had no idea what Jake's last name happened to be. Totally tack-balls, that was.

"It's really new, may end up being nothing. Let's not jinx it?"

She sighed, frowning a little. "It's very unusual for me, but I took to you almost immediately after meeting you at the cancer benefit. Part of that was certainly due to Caroline

Sparks raving about you—I've always found her to be an excellent judge of character—but beyond that, I just liked you instantly."

"That's very sweet and right back at ya. Please don't take this the wrong the way, but I imagine it isn't always easy for someone in your position to find friends."

She laughed, sounding slightly jaded, taking a moment to smooth over a crease in her pants.

"Don't get me wrong, I come from humble beginnings, and I'm motivated and driven by that, but I can't imagine what it must be like to be Julia Freeman-Kingsley."

"It's a lot of pressure some days," she said, cheekily.

"I would imagine it would be, oppressively so?"

She cocked her head to the side like she might be surprised he'd said that. "You're very sweet, I think."

Before he could respond, they each turned hearing a commotion coming from the hall.

"Confounded woman, I have no intention of taking off my damn shoes!"

Julia rolled her eyes dramatically. "It's okay Ilsa, we'll let grumpy-puss keep his shoes on. So help me we'll never hear the end of it, otherwise!"

Levi did his best to hold back his laughter picturing the tiny woman who had let him though the front door trying to body-block the senator.

"He really is the worst." Julia sighed.

"You do realize that it's bad for you to completely avoid germs, Julia," Senator Freeman said, marching across the living room to give his daughter a peck on the cheek. "It makes you weak, more susceptible to catching illness."

"We don't have time to stay long enough to make removing our shoes worthwhile, darling," Gloria Freeman said, smiling sweetly at her daughter before nodding an acknowledgement in Levi's direction.

Levi stood, ready to take the few steps required to offer his hand before Senator Freeman continued his rant.

"Just last week they featured a woman on the news who eats unwashed vegetables who has never been sick a day in her life. She eats them, dirt and all."

"Is that what you're doing now, Daddy, eating dirt in hopes of living a longer life?"

He shot her an irritated glare.

"Don't be ridiculous," Mrs. Freeman said to her daughter before smiling weakly at Levi. "We don't eat dirt."

"I'll make a note of that?" Levi asked, unsure if he was meant to take her seriously or not, which made Julia laugh.

"It's indecent to require your guests to remove their shoes, young lady."

Levi glanced down at his feet, wishing he could sit back down and shove them under the chair since he would no doubt be judged as weak for succumbing to Julia's wishes by having removed his own shoes.

"Gee, Daddy, tell me how you really feel?"

He sighed, taking a moment to give her one last glare of disapproval before succumbing to the pouty expression she offered in return, which finally put a smile on his sour puss.

"You're the most insolent of either of my children."

"You've said the same thing about both of us mind you," Julia said, winking at her father, who laughed heartily in response.

Julia made the appropriate introductions and they all took a seat except for Senator Freeman. When he'd begun poking around for intel on Harold and Gloria Freeman, Levi had heard from multiple sources that Harold was notorious for just this sort of thing. He was a big man, both in size and stature and he had an affinity for lording over others, especially during any type of negotiation. Levi took his actions now to be a positive sign and he remained seated, ensuring Harold could feel as if he were the one in control of this meeting.

"I must say that everyone is still raving about your work on the cancer ball last week," Gloria said, still smiling warmly, like a modern-day Doris Day.

There wasn't a hair out of place, Levi thought, admiring the overall packaging. Levi thanked her, having heard that this was also part of their shtick. She would butter you up, offering compliments while the senator came at you from the other side, bad-copping you into submission.

He had been prepared for this.

"She's not lying," Julia affirmed, "you are most certainly the talk of the town."

"It was a lovely evening, we had a glorious time, didn't we, darling?" Gloria asked.

The good senator grumbled some sort of an agreement. "A little too cold to be outdoors riding carousels and Ferris wheels, in my opinion."

Julia rolled her eyes, shaking her head behind her father's back.

"Donating your services was also a classy touch, Mr. Goode," Gloria added, placing her white-leather-gloved hand over her heart.

Gloria Freeman was a contradiction in terms, stunningly beautiful and immaculately put together, seemingly drawing people in with the warm, welcoming smile, while simultaneously making them feel inadequate with her perfect posture and impeccable manners.

"Of course, that wasn't a completely altruistic move on your part was it, son?" Harold asked, staring down at Levi as he slowly paced back and forth.

"Daddy," Julia scolded. "Really?"

Levi smiled at Julia, he couldn't manage to stop himself. "Naturally, assuming I did a good job and the benefit went smoothly, one could surmise that the benefits to me professionally speaking, would far outweigh any loss over the fee I waived when bidding on the event."

Harold looked smug all of sudden. "I would think so."

"That just makes me a good businessman, no?" Levi asked. "And for the record, I paid a great deal out of my own pocket to ensure that benefit was a truly special event—an evening no one who attended would soon forget."

"You've got spirit, I'll give you that, Mr. Goode, but enough of this chattering about the past. I'd like to hear what you've got planned for my baby girl's anniversary."

"Daddy, we really haven't had a chance to discuss—"

Harold held up his hand, signaling for Julia to stop talking. She made no attempt to disguise her irritation with her father's behavior.

"It's fine, Julia. That's certainly a fair question and while you and I haven't had the opportunity to sit down and discuss any specific details, just off the cuff, based upon my first impressions of you and after seeing your lovely home, I'm picturing something different from what you've done over the past several years—no disrespect to Libby. While the Tavern at the Mill is a gorgeous venue, its park adjacent location has always felt a little more wedding specific."

"I've never thought of that before, but you're right." Julia looked at her mother who appeared to be mulling that over before finally nodding that she also agreed with that assessment.

"Again, not knowing if Julia has any other locations in mind, I would probably recommend something that harkened back to the glamourous golden age of Wilde City in spirit, while not ignoring how far we've come since then. That begins with the event space, someplace with a history to rival that of your own, Senator. Someplace elegant that has played host to presidents, glamorous movie stars and even visiting European royalty—the Rainbow Palace."

The Rainbow Palace sat atop Wilde City Tower and had been the premier reigning nightclub and restaurant in the city for nearly a century.

"It's a grand idea, except for the fact they haven't closed down the entire place for a single event in decades."

"That's not completely accurate," Levi cut in. "They've closed the entire venue three times since the late eighties."

"With the size of our party, we'd need the whole place if we were going to fit."

"Leave that to me."

Harold scoffed, obviously unconvinced that Levi could deliver. Of course, Harold didn't know what Levi did, because the scandals of the so-called little-people were typically of no concern to the wealthy and elite—in spite of the fact they occupied the same space much of the time, they were very different worlds.

"I'm imagining the glitz and glamour of old Hollywood—lavish and lush with the romance of Gatsby. We inherently gain all of that with the location alone."

"And you believe you'd be able to secure the Rainbow Palace?" Gloria asked.

"I do indeed," Levi said.

"On such short notice?" Gloria pressed, obviously not believing it could be done.

"Regardless of one's station in life, everything always boils down to one simple, ever-fixed truth." Levi glanced between the Harold and Gloria. "It's all in who you know."

Harold puffed himself up and Gloria shot a sideways glance at her husband which Levi assumed to mean they were ready move in for the kill. He decided to cut them off at the path.

"Obviously, Julia was the first person to approach me after the Cancer Benefit, and as such, I'm inclined to offer her priority on any future dates."

"I get that you want to lock her in, son," Harold said, blustering a bit.

"Absolutely, and I can say with all honestly that I am dying to work with your daughter, sir. Candace Sparks has done nothing but sing Julia's praises." He could see the pride coming off the senator in waves. "Unfortunately we are on a bit of an ever-dwindling time line and on top of that, I've had two other offers to plan events that the same weekend which I've been putting off until after this meeting."

"Well, I'm not so sure we'll be able to commit without first speaking to one or two other event planners."

"I see." Levi cringed, while pretending to scribble something down in his notebook.

"Are we allowed to ask who these other clients might be?" Mrs. Freeman asked, smiling sweetly while attempting to put him on the spot.

Levi shrugged. "Considering they know I'm tentatively committed to Julia, I don't see why not."

"Only fair, after all," Mrs. Freeman added.

"I have a meeting penciled in with Titus Brewster for Monday morning—something about a company Christmas party, I believe." Levi paused, impressed that the good senator didn't so much as flinch, despite Levi knowing Brewster had been the number one contributor to Freeman's Democratic rival during the last, very heated election cycle.

Julia was biting down on her lip to keep herself from laughing, no doubt imagining smoke coming out of her father's ears.

Levi continued to play dumb. "That's more of a corporate thing, though, and in truth it doesn't hold as much interest for me as your event would. My other potential client is Rena Locklear." He paused, making eye contact with Mrs. Freeman. "I believe you two are friends, no?"

Julia's eyes widened like she might be unsure how her mother was likely to react in that moment.

Mrs. Freeman smiled warmly. "Of course, Rena… dear girl."

It was fairly well known that Gloria and Rena loathed one another, to the extent there had apparently been some sort of a physical altercation in the ladies powder room at the Fairmount Hills Country Club over the past summer.

Levi pretended like he knew none of that.

"Darling, considering Mr. Goode appears to be in such high demand and our dear Julia has her mind set so firmly on hiring him, I think it best if we acquiesce, don't you dear?"

"Whatever you think is best, darling," Senator Freeman said, as he walked over and reached out to shake Levi's hand.

Levi calmly stood and marveled at how quickly all the tension bled away from the man's face as they shook hands.

"We're very excited to be working with you, Mr. Goode, though I'm not going to sugar coat it for you. The Freemans aren't the easiest clan to work with."

"I am at your disposal, Senator, and Mrs. Freeman, I look forward to working with you as well."

"Good, that's just fine, young man, you send over a contract Monday morning and we can move forward with the planning from there."

Gloria stood, looking as cool and collected as she had upon arrival. "I'm afraid we've simply got to run, Julia."

"Of course, Mother, thank you for stopping by on your way to brunch. I'll walk you both out." Julia hugged her father as the two of them followed Gloria out of the room.

The instant they were out of sight Levi took a deep breath and sighed his relief over that meeting being history. His throat was suddenly very dry so he flopped back down into the chair and fished the bottle of water from his bag that was lying on the floor next to his feet. He forced himself to stop chewing on his lower lip, nervous that he may have taken things too far just then.

Still gulping down water when Julia walked back into the room, Levi looked up at her sheepishly.

"Oh. My. Goodness. I completely underestimated you, Mr. Levi Goode!" Julia squealed, sauntering back to the sofa to sit down.

He could feel his cheeks flush as he laughed under his breath. He shooed her away when she began to faux-bow down before him.

"You worked the two of them like a true master."

Levi started laughing, slightly embarrassed while still being proud of himself.

"First, buttering them up with all that Gatsby-American dynasty bit and then twisting the knife by taunting them with the possibility of losing out to the two people they each hate most in this world?"

Julia looked like she'd exhausted herself having doled out so much praise in such a short amount of time. "And I was worried they'd eat sweet little Levi alive."

He said nothing, just stared innocently back at her.

"You can cut the act with me, I'm legitimately impressed, Levi, seriously." Julia sighed, pulling a leg up and tucking it under the other. "It was like a master class in manipulation."

"Now you really flatter me," he finally said, fanning himself with his hand. "You don't think I went too far?"

"I think you rode the line beautifully, and while you appeared to be completely clueless, you can bet your bottom dollar my mother will be checking you out after bringing up Rena. You made that vein in her forehead pop out when you mentioned her name. She was going to hire you after that no matter what, if only to keep Rena from getting you."

"You need to air this joint out lady," a man's voice called out from somewhere behind Levi. "I assume I just missed our loathsome parents as I smell the faint scent of disappointment and judgment hanging in the air?"

Julia squealed, flying up off the sofa and sprinting across the room.

Levi turned in time to see her nearly tackle-hug one man, while a second one stood a few feet farther back looking vaguely uncomfortable. Levi stood, and began collecting his things, assuming Julia just received some unexpected company.

His heart stopped the instant she took a few steps back revealing Paramedic Jake standing there, smiling warmly at

Julia. She pinched his cheeks while hopping up and down like a giddy schoolgirl. The instant their gaze met, Jake's smile faded slightly and Levi decided to go with the assumption it was due to shock more than actual disappointment.

"Hello, Victor, glad to have you back safe and sound," Julia said to the other man who was with Jake before seeming to notice that Jake was still staring at Levi. "I'm so rude, my apologies, Levi."

Levi smiled but couldn't manage any actual words. He'd been obsessing over the fact Jake hadn't called him since their so-called movie date and now here he was, in the last place he'd ever expected to see the man.

"This is my twin brother, Jake, and his husband, Victor," Julia said, introducing them.

Levi's head started to spin and he glanced down at his chest, certain someone had just plunged a dagger straight through his heart. He knew he'd heard her correctly, despite his brain attempting to work out any other potential possibilities.

His is Myan Jake and his foosball Victor?

Tis my twin brethren Jackson is buzzed-end tic-tar?

Dismay twins other Jake's end-cussed-clicker?

Unfortunately everything he came up with made no sense, but then, what he thought he'd heard her say didn't make sense either. His Jake couldn't possibly have a husband. Paramedic Jake was not the kind of guy who would go out looking for random movie dates with single men when he already had a man waiting for him back at home?

"Are you all right?" Julia asked, ripping Levi out of his inner rant.

"Think I just stood up too fast," he said, frowning upon the realization that that made zero sense, so he added.

"Probably forgot to eat lunch and had five or six too many coffees."

"Let Jake look at you, he's an EMT."

"No!" Levi yelled, staring back at the three of them who were startled by the outburst. "I mean, like, totally not necessary. I'll just get out of your hair so you can visit with your brother and his *husband.*"

Jake's eyes closed for one or two seconds too long to be considered blinking. Part of Levi would've loved nothing more than pointing a finger in the man's face while screaming *cheater!*, but not enough of him that he was willing to fuck up the massive commission he would receive upon completion of the Freeman-Kingsley anniversary extravaganza—which would undoubtedly further cement him as the new party planner/event organizer extraordinaire in Wilde City.

Cheater-butt was not going to fuck this opportunity up for him!

Cheater-butt could sit around fretting over whether or not Levi was going to fuck up his entire world at any moment by telling his husband that Jake was in fact, a cheesy-ass, cheater-butt!

Cheater-butt needed to stop looking at him that way with those fucking cheatery-blue eyes of self-proclaimed innocence!!!

"Let me get the cook to rustle you up something to eat," Julia insisted. "We've got loads of party-talk to discuss and I'd love to have my baby brother weigh in as well."

Before allowing him the opportunity to object, Julia turned and fled the room, leaving Levi alone with Jake and his stupid husband, both of whom he was attempting to stare down with the death-ray eyes he wished he'd had, in that moment.

Levi likely would have found Victor attractive had he not been the current cause of the stabbing sensation in his head and chest. He was a big guy, beefy, but very well-manicured in an Anderson Cooper kind of way—groomed within an inch of his life—the epitome of business casual, dressed in light grey dress pants and a navy cotton pull-over.

All Levi wanted to do was run over and mess up Victor's hair. Albeit a particularly infantile reaction, but the thought of doing so made him feel a teensy bit better as the shock began to wear off and his anger began to really kick into high gear.

"I'm going to run to the restroom, babe," Victor said, tapping at the screen of his smart phone, not even bothering to offer any sort of greeting to Levi.

What an ass-hat! Look at me…, I'm so busy and important that I don't have time to look up from my phone and be a decent human being.

"Okay, sure," Jake said quietly, not taking his eyes off of Levi, who was admittedly spiraling into an anger-ball of epic proportions over the absolute betrayal of it all.

Before he managed to get a single word out, Jake was shaking his head and holding up a hand as if that might somehow stop the words from coming out.

"I can't believe you're *married!*" Levi hissed.

"Technically, gay marriage isn't legal here yet, so the accurate statement would be that I have a boyfriend."

Levi reared his head back in complete shock and awe.

"Not an important distinction," Jake said. "I see that now."

"Why?" Levi asked, "I mean… like, *why?*"

"First of all, nothing really happened between us."

"You almost kissed me."

Jake swallowed, wincing at that. "Almost doesn't count."

"You had your hand between my legs," Levi pointed out.

"Completely innocently, let me remind you," Jake said.

"I can't believe you're going to stand there and act like nothing was going on between the two of us that night."

Jake's forehead crinkled up and he ran the palm of his hand over his face.

"Why did you even come to the theatre?"

"I… I don't know, damn it," Jake admitted, tossing his arms into the air. "Honestly, Levi, I do not know why. I showed up because I enjoyed meeting you—thought perhaps we might make good friends."

"Oh puh-lease, you don't almost kiss your friends."

"That may be true, but I didn't show up there intending to kiss you, damn it. But after the movie… I don't know what happened."

"Whatever, like I can believe anything you say at this point."

"I am sorry, Levi, I promise that I never intended to lead you on." Jake glanced back to see if his sister or boyfriend were anywhere within earshot. "You're funny and you made me laugh. Add Miss Ruby to the equation and I wanted to get to know you—that's it. That's all I know for sure to be true. It was just a movie for Christ's sake. Then you had to go and look at me with those pleading, kiss me eyes, and I lost myself for a moment."

"So it's *my* fault?" Levi asked, shaking his head. "You're a real peach."

"Do you guys know each other?" Julia asked, coming back into the room followed by Victor who was hot on her heels and finally found a reason to tear himself away from his phone.

"Sort of," Jake said.

"He was the paramedic called to my mother's house earlier this week."

"Oh my God," Julia said, her face going white. "She's okay, your mother?"

"Yes, sorry, Julia—didn't mean to freak you out there. My mom is totally okay."

She looked at her brother as if needing his confirmation that all was well.

Jake nodded.

"Glad to hear that," Victor said, sidling up next to Jake while shoving his phone into his pocket. "My hero once again saving the day, huh?"

"Wasn't really one of those life-threatening situations, babe," Jake said, no doubt doing his best to avoid further attention being aimed his direction.

Levi rubbed at his chest, hearing Jake refer to Victor as *babe,* making it difficult to breathe. He glanced down at his bag, which chirped, signaling he had a message.

"I should take that actually. Make sure it's nothing urgent with my mother."

"Of course." Julia motioned he could step into the next room if he liked.

He wasted no time, grabbing his bag off the floor and deciding he needed to get the fuck out of here as soon as possible. He was way too pissed to be able to hide it indefinitely and at the same time, Levi was second guessing himself. Maybe Jake was right. It was Levi who had made more out of going to the movies than he should have? Maybe it was he alone who had inadvertently attempted to turn something completely innocent on Jake's part into something he'd never intended it to be?

Was it wrong that Jake almost kissed him? Absolutely! But Jake may have been telling the truth. They'd never referred to it as a date, and really, did a movie without the accompanying dinner even qualify as a date? Or was it just a movie?

Either way he came at the situation, Levi ended up being the buffoon, and that made him feel like a complete shit.

Fishing his cell out of his leather messenger bag, he noticed a missed call from Ruby and two texts from Valerie, who wanted him to come out with her to Wilde City's premiere drag club, the Masquerade de Cabaret, later that night.

"Not a chance, Val," he muttered, redialing the missed call from Momma.

"Hey, sorry I missed your call, Mom, what's up?"

Jake was staring at him from the other room and Julia noticed, turning to see what Jake was looking at. He waved at the two of them before turning away.

"I'm calling because the nurse never showed up this morning and I wanted to tell you so I don't get blamed for it."

"Are you sure you shouldn't be blamed for it?"

"I barely know this one, for Christ's sake. I haven't even had time to decide whether I like her or not."

He glanced at his watch. "It's nearly one-thirty, momma, so why am I now just hearing about this?"

"Good grief, I took a nap so I'm a little late realizing that she isn't here."

He sighed, shaking his head. "Well, I'm coming out to stay with you for the rest of the weekend. Monday morning we'll see what can be done to find you a replacement."

"I'm perfectly capable of taking care of myself, Levi. Let's not forget which one of us is the parent and who is the child."

"Agreed, Ruby, so please start acting your age for once and stop fighting me at each and every turn. Contrary to what you think, I'm not trying to steal your independence from you. I'm doing everything I can to ensure you're able to maintain it, but that is going to require your cooperation. You cannot continue to live alone, that is a fact. I know you don't want to leave your home, but if you continue to run off everyone I hire, I'll be forced to move you into my loft with me."

"That's not going to happen," Ruby said flatly.

"We can discuss this further when I get there, okay?"

"Fine."

"Do you need anything?" he asked, feeling bad for making her angry.

"A more sympathetic and understanding son wouldn't fucking hurt."

Levi laughed. "You're a real piece a work."

"Goodbye," she said, before hanging up on him.

He sighed, turning around to find Jake standing a few feet away.

"We need to talk."

"I'm going to have to go," Levi said, forcing himself to stop chewing on his lip.

"Your mom?" Julia asked, coming up behind Jake.

"Unfortunately, yes. Her home health nurse didn't show up so I'm going to have to go stay with her until Monday."

Jake smiled, and Levi knew he was operating under the assumption Ruby had run off another nurse.

"You can wipe that smile away, mister, it's not funny."

Julia's eyes widened slightly.

"She's quite a character," Jake said, clarifying things for Julia.

"She's diabolical." Levi lifted the strap of his bag onto his shoulder. "Rain check on the party talk?"

"Absolutely," Julia said. "You can pop by for dinner one night this week, perhaps?"

"You've got a date," Levi said, awkwardly glancing at Jake, whose eyebrow hitched as if to say, *So you make everything into a date, I see.*

"Give Ruby my best," Jake said.

Levi smiled but made no promises he'd do anything of the sort considering he wasn't all that sure Jake's so-called 'best' was good enough for his mother at this point.

CHAPTER FIVE

Monday morning had rolled around way too quickly, Levi thought, glancing at his watch. It was a little after ten and he was already yearning for five o'clock to roll around. Not a good sign considering how much work there was to do.

The building that housed Goode City Event & Party Planning had been built in 1867. The entire waterfront, including the boardwalk and most of the docklands, had burned to the ground several years before. Following the fire, cast-iron, brick and stone had become the building materials of choice, and while most of the buildings throughout the six block area grew in height, the advent of the more modern day skyscrapers had still been several decades away.

The main floor featured large, arched storefront windows that looked out over the cobblestone street toward the large boardwalk and piers just beyond. Sixteen foot high ceilings provided an airy, spacious feel to the otherwise narrow interior. The original copper ceiling tiles had been stripped and restored back to their original luster as had the wood floors, which still creaked when he walked across them—something that initially annoyed him—though he'd since grown to love it, deciding it was the building's way of speaking to him. A solid wood carved retail counter sat just inside the front door along the north wall, and had been converted into a reception desk.

Now I just need to hire a receptionist, he thought, staring blankly at the wisp of a girl currently seated across the boardroom table from him and Valerie.

They'd been trapped inside the glass-walled conference room all morning long, as the onslaught of potential new hire interviews continued—for what Valerie referred to as her minions. It was the last thing he wanted to be doing, while Valerie appeared to be enjoying herself immensely— her favorite part being the subsequent trashing of each candidate as soon as they left the room. She was completely cutthroat, and while her opinions weren't necessarily incorrect, she could have found kinder turns-of-phrases for the poor unfortunate souls, if she'd tried. Of course that would require extra effort on her part, so Levi wasn't even going to bother asking.

In truth, he was more than a little bitter, still stinging from the knowledge that Jake Freeman, the man of his dreams, belonged to someone else. He felt it like a slap across the face as he continued replaying the scene over and over in the back of his mind as Julia introduced him to her twin brother, Jake… *and his stupid husband!*

Levi was completely devastated and depressed, which was kind of idiotic considering: one, he barely knew Jake; and two, he was a grown ass man, and as such, should have matured beyond the post-pubescent, Tammy-Tragic, overtly emo stage many, many moons ago. Instead, he sat there staring blankly out into space, barely paying attention to the people they were interviewing. Worst of all, Levi found himself looking forward to the moment each person walked out of the room so he could feed off the evil commentary Valerie spouted off like some sort of sicko-succubus.

It was horrible and Levi was aware that he was spiraling.

He knew that attempting to concentrate on the interviews was a complete waste of time so he just sat there, feeling wretched with a fake-ass smile plastered onto his face. The one good thing that had happened today was finding a temporary nurse to look after Ruby until something more permanent could be worked out.

As it turned out, spending the weekend with his mommy had made for a nice distraction. Ruby had been able to sense something was off with him, but she never pressured him for details. She was good like that. Instead, she kept him distracted by sitting with him on the sofa, binge-watching old movie musicals for a day and a half.

Smiling at the young woman who got up from the conference table, Levi stood, seeing Valerie do the same out of the corner of his eye. He reached out, shaking her hand. "Very nice meeting you."

"We'll be in touch," Valerie added, giving him an odd sideways look.

"Awesome, thank you," she said, breathily, "really great meeting you both. I've heard great things about your great company."

She sort of curtsied, before seeming to realize what she was doing and then turned and ran out of the room.

"That was…"

"Fucking weird," Valerie clarified.

"She did just curtsy, right? I didn't imagine that?"

"No, you didn't." Valerie sniffed, taking her application and turning it over onto the 'No' pile. "That bitch be crazy."

"Was she having an asthma attack?" Levi asked, sitting back down, trying not to think about Jake and failing miserably. He hated this feeling, like he was losing out on something, and as a result, the rest of his life was going to totally suck.

"I don't know what her problem was, but I would murder her if I had to listen to that weird breathy voice talking at me all day long."

"Word." Levi nodded while blankly staring out at the line of people they still had to interview. He wanted to go upstairs, put his PJ's back on and crawl into bed

"Like stab her in the fucking face, you know?" Valerie asked.

"Mmm hmm," Levi said with a sigh.

"Like this." She began air-stabbing at his face, making that Alfred Hitchcock screechy Psycho movie sound effect.

Levi jerked back, staring at her like she'd lost her freakin' mind. "What the hell are you doing?"

Pushing her chair back, Valerie walked around the side of the table "Just as I thought, you're not even listening to me anymore."

"I...am." Levi decided it safest to sit back down and not make any sudden movements.

"No, if you'd been listening you would have understood my face stabbing gesture."

"Oh, I understood it."

She made this really loud, very annoying game show buzzer sound before pointing at him. "Liar, liar, pants on fire!"

"You do know they can all see us, right?" Levi asked, waving out at the dozen or more people sitting in the lobby area of the office in order to illustrate this fact for her.

A few of the people sitting in the lobby area waved back at him, looking confused as they glanced back and forth at one another trying to figure out who Levi was attempting to communicate with.

He was seriously rethinking the whole glass-pane-walled-in conference room, which had seemed like a good choice at the time, allowing all the natural light from the storefront windows to filter to the back of the space.

"What's your point?" Valerie asked, apparently unable to make the connection on her own.

"That making crazy, stabby motions at one another might not send the right message about what it's like to work here to all of the no doubt now completely freaked out interviewees?"

She stood there mulling that over for a few moments. "Fair enough."

Levi propped his elbows up onto the table and planted his face into the palms of his hands.

"I'll go get the next one," she said greedily, as if nothing in the world was more exciting to her.

He groaned into his hands, hearing the door swish open and closed, thankful for whatever precious few moments of peace and quiet he was going to get. His head was beginning to throb, which seemed about par for the course. Looking out over the back part of the office space, he noticed all the decorations he'd purchased for the cancer benefit stacked up against the far wall, including the seventy-seven eight foot Victorian-themed canvas carnival backdrops which had been laid out flat and stacked on top of one another.

Why Valerie hadn't had the men he'd hired to move the stuff, unload it into the back storage area, where it belonged he had yet to ask—assuming instead she'd been too distracted ogling the sweaty, muscled mover beefcake to think clearly.

Then there was the mountainous pile of phone messages from potential clients he and Val still hadn't completely sorted through. He glanced down at the three piles of applications Val had laying on the table, praying that the thicker stack was the 'no' pile and not the 'still waiting to be interviewed' pile. They had so much work to do and they desperately needed to hire some help if they were going to make a go of it. That knowledge didn't prevent him from sneering at the piles, struggling to think back over the faces that had sat across the table from them throughout the morning for even one that stood out.

All he could see was Jake's face. *Stupid, cheater-butt, face.*

He shook his head, wishing he'd never met the fucking asshole.

His business was finally taking off like a rocket. This was what he had wanted—what he had worked so hard for over the past year. He could not allow this Jake disappointment to ruin the rest of his life.

So I'll end up an old maid, or whatever the gay dude equivalent of that happened to be.

Always the bridesmaid and never the bridegroom.

The Susan Lucci of love.

He recalled Valerie's kitty comment from the night of the benefit and sneered. "The cats are a fucking no go, though. Gotta draw the line somewhere."

By the time Valerie came back into the room, Levi looked up, seeing that the lobby was practically empty as the last few people were walking out the door. He immediately began to fear the worst.

"Don't worry, I didn't do anything bad. I did however send everyone home—well, all except one—he's a total hottie! Even though it's very apparent you are in no mood for interviewing new employees today, I have no intention of allowing you and your issues to get in the way of me ogling some sexy beefcake for however long I can stretch out this one final interview."

He smiled, sitting back in his chair and remembering why he put up with all her other shenanigans. When push came to shove she always had his back... well, sorta.

"As grateful as I am for you doing that, I feel horrid, Val. Those people took time out of their day and spent money getting here."

"End of the day, you're not really here though, are you?" Val asked.

Levi shook his head.

"Then I did them a favor. Besides, I made appointments for the rest of them, sprinkled throughout the week, so they all have set times to come back, which means no sitting around for hours waiting for their turn."

"Well, that is nice, I hate waiting."

"I'm well aware, you little diva."

He scowled at her, and then stuck out his tongue, which she seemed to appreciate, not surprisingly.

"Bring on the hottie so we can get this over with and get on with our day."

"He's in the restroom, so just settle down there."

Levi scoffed. "He can't urinate on his own time?"

"Listen here, boss man, this relationship of ours can only work if I remain the snarky, inappropriately selfish one, you dig?"

He laughed, finding that humorous instead of horrifying... which a sure sign that the apocalypse was upon them.

They each plastered on smiles as Valerie's hottie came out of the restroom, looking mildly embarrassed to see they were waiting on him. As he strode into the conference room, Levi had to admit the man was definitely easy on the eyes. Too young looking for Levi's taste, but still studly all the same.

Valerie introduced him as Angelo Salazar. It seemed fitting that he had a name that was every bit as unique and easy to remember as the man himself was. Dark eyes, wavy ink-black, shiny hair and flawless, sun-kissed Mediterranean looking skin all combined to make Angelo one of the single prettiest men Levi had ever seen. He looked like he belonged on a runway in Milan—that perfect mix of delicate features and high cheekbones packaged in an otherwise mouth-watering, masculine frame.

Valerie was smiling like a newly crowned beauty queen when she came around the table and took her seat next to Levi. As she began the interview, discussing his previous work experience and whatnot, Levi found himself becoming sadder over the fact he couldn't stop thinking about Jake.

"We do a lot of evening events, naturally," Valerie said, "and oftentimes have to step outside of typical roles within the company—"

"Mmm," Levi nodded, only half paying attention at this point, "very true."

If a man that was as gorgeous as Angelo couldn't manage to make Levi forget about every other man on the planet, including Jake-fucking-Freeman, there was a serious problem brewing. It was a frightening thought that now had Levi completely freaked.

"Occasionally, we also organize private events that require staff, bartenders and waiters to be shirtless. Would that be a problem for you?" Valerie asked.

Levi scowled, wondering what the hell she was talking about. He started to interject when an even more terrifying thought crept into his brain. What if there truly was only one other person out there for everyone? Obviously, not everyone waited for or found their perfect *one*, which would certainly explain the divorce rate in this country. But if there was a *one* for everyone and if his *one* were Jake, Levi was screwed, because Jake hadn't waited for him like he had Jake!

What an asshole!

Levi looked over at Valerie, half expecting a high-five as she yelled, "Hell yeah… he's a total asshole!"

Instead he found her looking up at a shirtless Angelo, who was smiling and laughing right along with her from across the table as he turned, providing a mouth-watering 360 degree view of his well-muscled physique.

"Oh my God!" Levi shot up from his seat, startling the two of them.

His arms began flailing as his foot caught on a chair leg, before getting tangled up with one another. Before he could say the words, *sexual harassment lawsuit*, he was falling backward, unable to grab a hold of the table, or the chair which was already lying on its side, or Valerie who actually recoiled from him instead of reaching out to try and prevent him from ending up on his ass.

Levi closed his eyes, expecting the pain to reverberate through his body the instant he hit the hardwoods. He grunted, rather indelicately, feeling a pair of sturdy arms around his back. Realizing he was no longer suffering the effects of gravity, he opened one eye to see Angelo staring down at him.

"I got ya," Angelo said, slowing lifting him back up to his feet.

Levi was mortified, naturally, even more so after whispering, "Damn, you smell good."

Angelo started laughing, finally letting go of Levi but refusing to vacate his air space. "Thank you for the lovely, albeit unusual compliment."

Valerie looked pissed, staring at the floor like she was considering throwing herself across the room in hopes Angelo would rescue her as well.

Levi took several steps back, needing some distance from the Angelo-scent and sights before him. "My deepest apologies for my associate's rude, objectifying behavior."

"I don't mind." Angelo winked at Levi, a cocky smile sitting comfortably across his face. "Though I was a little insulted over the fact it took you so long to take notice of all this."

Levi's mouth fell open slightly, unsure how to respond to that.

"I work out… like a lot."

Levi laughed, somehow catching on that he was both flirting with him and kidding around.

"Obviously you're hired."

"Yay!!" Valerie said, clapping. "Sexy minion."

Angelo looked at her funny. "You're a bit of an odd bird aren't you?"

"Ignore her please… and you can put your shirt back on, please, sorry again that *anyone* asked you to undress."

He smirked. "Too distracting for you to take now that you finally noticed, I get it."

Levi shook his head, sneaking one last peek as Angelo slipped his shirt back on, tucking it back inside the waistband of his pants.

"As I was saying before…" Angelo frowned, visibly confused over the best way to reference Levi's outburst, "…your episode?"

Levi nodded begrudgingly, deciding that was probably the kindest descriptor he was likely to get.

"I've done a little bit of everything over the past year and a half since relocating to Wilde City, so I'm totally open to whatever. It would be great to find one job instead of getting shuffled around the city doing temp work to make ends meet."

"That's great to hear, Angelo," Levi said, setting his chair back upright as they each sat back down. "The fact you're willing to jump in and do anything is great for us, and having some extra muscle around wouldn't suck."

"Indeed-e-oh," Valerie whispered, her beauty-queen smile once again firmly in place.

"Awesome!" Angelo said, looking considerably younger when overly excited. "When do I start?"

"When can you start?" Valerie asked.

"Right now if you need me," he said.

"Tomorrow would be fine," Levi said, turning toward the lobby and catching movement out of the corner of his eye.

Jake waved at him, smiling sheepishly as the front door closed behind him. He pointed toward the chairs, indicating he would be taking a seat as opposed to turning back around and vacating the premises.

"What time would you like me here?" Angelo asked.

"Eight would be—"

"Nine o'clock would be perfect," Levi said, unable to tear his gaze away from Jake.

"Or nine, that would be fine as well," Valerie said.

"Huh?" Levi asked, seeing Valerie stare daggers at him. "Oh, sorry Val."

"No problem, nine will allow us some time to get organized in the morning before you show up."

"Good thinking," Levi said, turning back to see Jake staring at him.

"If you need to go take care of that, we can finish up here without you," Val said.

"Right," Levi said, laughing awkwardly as he stood from the table and shook Angelo's hand. "Welcome aboard."

"Thank you, Mr. Goode," Angelo said.

"Levi will do just fine," he added, leaving them to it.

* * * *

As he rounded the corner of the conference room and slowly headed to where Jake was seated, that instant ache returned, making him wonder why Jake had showed up here when he'd made it pretty clear he hadn't ever wanted to see him again.

Jake stood, apparently able to read the lack of enthusiasm on Levi's face.

"I know I shouldn't be here, Levi, and I apologize for showing up unannounced, but I couldn't stand to let another day go by with you hating me."

"I don't hate you, Jake," Levi said matter-of-factly.

"You sure as shit don't like me," Jake interjected, cringing when Levi didn't jump in with any denials. "I need to talk to you, explain my side so you don't think I'm a completely evil asshole."

That irritated him, because frankly, Levi needed to think of him as an evil asshole and if the man had any ounce of chivalry he'd have already realized that and left him be.

"So who's the guy?" Jake asked, nudging his head toward the conference room.

Levi turned to see Angelo was watching them, waving at them before returning to the paperwork Valerie had him filling out.

"He works here, Jake," Levi said, offering no further information. "Is that what you came here for, to interrogate me about my business?"

Jake sighed, shaking his head. "Of course not. Look, could we get out of here? Let me buy you a coffee."

"You're not afraid I'll accidently assume it's a date?" Levi asked sarcastically.

"I deserve that," Jake said, lifting up his hands in surrender.

"This really isn't a good time for me," Levi said.

Jake reached over and took his hand. "Please, Levi, give me thirty minutes of your time." He lifted Levi's hand, checking the time on his watch before letting go of him. "I've gotta be at work in little over an hour, so I can't keep you too long."

Levi nodded, mildly disgusted with himself for relenting. "Let me go grab my phone and keys," he said, turning to find Valerie standing there holding both.

"Bye bye," she said sweetly.

He mouthed the words *behave yourself* and shot her a nasty look that said he meant business.

"Hi, I'm Jake," he said, offering his hand to Val before Levi began shoving him toward the door.

"There's no need for introductions, Jake," Levi said.

"You might feel differently—"

"Do you still have a boyfriend?" Levi asked, following Jake out on to the sidewalk.

"Yeah," Jake said, scowling.

Levi smiled, petting his shoulder like a puppy in need of training. "Then I won't change my mind."

Jake sneered, apparently not appreciating that answer. Levi could also spot the man's determination to prove him wrong, which frustrated him all the more.

* * * *

By the time they'd waited in line and eventually placed their order, a good fifteen minutes had blown by, which Levi decided was a point scored for his side. He knew this wasn't a game—that real people with real feelings could potentially get hurt by whatever happened here. However, Levi was also aware that he was one of those potential victims, and for whatever reason, the whole keeping score thing seemed to help.

The fact that he couldn't look Jake in the face without wishing he could lunge over the table and maul him—in the best possible sense—was a point for Jake's side. The thing that bugged Levi more than anything was that damn feeling he couldn't shake telling him that Jake wasn't the monster Levi needed him to be.

A guy that sped all over the city trying to save people's lives, couldn't possibly be a complete monster.

A guy who had been so kind to Ruby, continually reassuring her that she was going to be okay and then going one step further by checking in on her while she was staying in the hospital? Not very monster-like.

A guy that made Levi yearn for all the things he'd not so carefully shoved to the side in order to make way for his career and the creation of his business?

"Anti-monstery," Levi mumbled.

"What was that?" Jake asked, taking a seat across from him at the tiny table crammed into the tight corner next to the bathroom which Levi had specifically selected because it was the least romantic setting he could find after surveying the entire café.

"Nothing, I said nothing."

Jake tapped out a quick text while shooting Levi a sideways glance as if to say he wasn't buying it. "Apologies for the texting, just letting my partner know where to pick me up."

Levi smirked wondering if it wasn't some other dude he'd dated and dashed on.

"Let's get on with it, times a tickin'." Levi pointed to his watch. "Say what you've gotta say."

"I love that you still wear a watch," Jake said.

"Lots of people still wear watches," Levi said, correcting him.

"Do they?" he asked. "Aside from old men?"

"This is what you brought me here for?" Levi asked, wide-eyed.

"No, of course not, sheesh—just trying to segway into the tougher stuff, my apologies… again."

Levi sighed, wishing he didn't feel the need to be quite so acidic. "I'm sorry."

"No, Levi, I'm the one who is sorry. I should have told you about Victor before showing up at the movies that night."

"Why didn't you?" Levi asked.

"Honestly, things have been a little rocky the past few years with Victor. The way you looked at me, I could tell you were into me, which is exactly why I should have told you and also exactly the reason why I didn't."

Levi shrugged. "I'm confused."

"It's been a while since anyone has looked at me like that."

"I seriously doubt that."

"Okay, well… a long time since it came from someone I wanted to look at me that way."

"Oh."

Now that he finally understood he wished he didn't. He took a sip of coffee and watched as Jake did the same.

"I'd like to be able to say that came out wrong, but really it's the truth, which just happens to make me look like a shit-heel."

Levi grinned, never having heard anyone use that term aside from he and Ruby.

"I wasn't out looking for trade." Jake was careful to clarify. "I have never done that. You just happened."

Levi nodded, thinking this version of events sounded more like the type of guy he imagined Jake to be after meeting him.

"If it's any consolation to you, were I not already with someone, I'd be so into you, Levi. I wouldn't give you so much as a moment to catch your breath in my attempt to sweep you off your feet." Jake sighed and glanced out the window, as if he knew it was true but still didn't like it, as if the mere act of saying the words had left a bad taste in his mouth.

There was the knife in the gut, slicing straight through him as the future he'd imagined with Jake turned into some alternate universe that this version of himself would never live to see.

Jake smiled, tapping on Levi's hand trying to draw his attention back. "Beyond any attraction, I do genuinely like you as a person. You're funny and sweet and I don't know about you, but I don't really have many friends, even fewer who are gay men, and I miss that."

"So you wanna be friends with me?" Levi asked, thinking that couldn't be right. Not after the things he'd just said.

"Growing up the way I did, it was tough to meet someone new only to eventually discover they only wanted to be around me because of my family."

"Poor little rich boy, huh?"

Jake flinched, like that may have truly wounded him. Levi was surprised that he felt every bit as good over thinking he'd hurt Jake as he did bad for doing the same. He caught a twinge of the achy-chest again, so he glanced down at his coffee, deciding another drink might break the awkwardness.

"I'm not wealthy, Levi, my parents are and the instant I decided not to be the person they wanted me to be, I was on my own—have been ever since. I have a small nest egg from money that was left to me when my grandfather passed away, but otherwise, I live on what I earn working."

"Sorry, I didn't know that. Regardless, it's not my place to pass judgment over you even if you were Richie Rich."

Jake smiled sheepishly. "So, can we be friends?"

"I don't know." Levi sucked down the last of his coffee. "Part of me thinks this friend thing is a terrible idea."

Jake nodded, looking down at the table like his worst fears had just been realized.

Levi wanted to punch him and hug him all at the same time.

"But if I'm being completely honest with myself, I don't really have many friends either." Levi said the words easily enough, yet he didn't enjoy the sense of loneliness they left behind. "That being said, Jake, I really hate being lied to and it pisses me off every time I think about it."

"I'm very sorry, Levi. I swear to you that I don't run around trying to hook up with guys when my boyfriend is out of town. I am not that guy."

Levi hated hearing Jake say the 'B' word. "I do like you, but I need to think about this, okay?"

Jake frowned but nodded that he understood.

In truth, Levi was unsure if he would ever be able to get beyond the disappointment that he could never be with Jake. The thought of being around the man and not being able to reach out and take his hand or kiss him—that wrecked his insides. He'd have to truly be some sort of an emotional masochist to sign up for a friendship like that.

Jake reached over, placing a hand over Levi's, giving it a firm squeeze, apologizing once more before pulling away and getting up from the table. He said goodbye before walking out the door and hopping into a massive black pickup that had pulled up outside the café.

The instant Jake was gone Levi wanted him back. That made him incredibly sad and he decided right then, there was no way he could be friends with Jake.

He grabbed his cell off the table and tapped on the screen, pulling up the text he'd received from Jake last week letting him know what room Ruby was in at the hospital. Levi stared at the phone, conflicted because Ruby had made sure he was aware of the fact Jake had gone above and beyond that day, making sure one of the nurses texted him the room number so he could pass that information along to Levi personally.

Again, not the actions of your typical asshole.

He shook his head, frustrated, then he sighed.

Levi typed out a quick message and hesitated briefly, finger hovering over the screen as part of him was screaming for him to not hit the 'send' button.

Levi closed his eyes and tapped the screen, sitting there quietly for a moment before re-opening his eyes to a new reality—one that wasn't going to include Jake Freeman.

CHAPTER SIX

Jake slipped on his seatbelt, hearing his phone chirp, alerting him to the fact he had a text. He settled into the seat as Craig pulled away from the curb and sped off down the street, weaving in and out of traffic. "Do you have to drive like a crazy person?"

He went fishing through his coat pocket for his phone.

"Wasn't that the orgy guy?" Craig asked, completely ignoring the one about his driving.

Jake shot him a look.

"What? His name is Levi and we're fr—" Jake felt sick to his stomach reading the text message from Levi. "*Not* going to be friends."

"You look disappointed."

"I am, actually." Jake shoved the phone back in his pocket.

"It's not the phone's fault." Craig slammed on the brakes as the light changed before he was able to speed through the stoplight.

"Try telling that to your brake pads," Jake mumbled, receiving a grimace from Craig for his trouble.

"You still have me as a friend, baby," Craig reminded him.

"Yeah, I know, right back at ya." He sighed, pulling the phone out so he could read the text again. "I really liked him."

"He really liked you, I think." Craig started grinning, looking particularly devilish. "In a wanna shove his face in your crotch kinda way."

"Don't even go there."

"You telling me that you didn't want to go there?" Craig asked. "Why go to the movies with the guy, then?"

"I have a boyfriend, lest you've forgotten that fact."

"I try to forget that fact every day."

"Why are you so hard on Victor?"

"He's fine, I suppose." Craig shrugged, keeping his eyes on the road. "If you're into that sort of thing."

"Really?" Jake asked, cringing as Craig weaved in and around several cars. "That's the best you can do?"

"Look I can't help it, the man is a bit of snob."

Jake sighed. "I know he can be a little tough to take at times."

"A little?" Craig cursed under his breath as he swerved to miss a bike messenger.

"He's never been anything but nice to you." No matter how many times he read the text message Jake couldn't manage to suss out any sort of clue or opening that led him to believe Levi might be open to discussing things further. "Fucking hate texts."

"Put the phone away and stop obsessing over your wanna-be lover's text message and try concentrating on the topic at hand—your boyfriend? And I'm pretty sure that where Vic is concerned, you're confusing tolerance with kindness."

"There is a nice guy underneath all the… stuff, you know that, right?"

"If you say so." Craig held up a hand like he was ready to surrender the topic.

"Damn, I knew you weren't Victor's biggest fan, but I never knew you truly disliked him." Jake could tell his partner was a bit embarrassed judging by his uncomfortable looking posture, and the slight flush in his cheeks.

"I'm sorry. And he's not that bad, never explicitly rude. But whenever I'm around Victor, I can't shake the feeling he's counting down the minutes, like I'm a social obligation or something. It's like he's made up some arbitrarily appropriate allotment of time in which he feels obligated to spend talking to me and he's got his eye on the timer, watching that clock just praying for it to be over already." Craig steered the truck through a short maze of other cars, making a quick left turn as the light was changing. "It's not just me, either, Jake. Sophia's noticed it as well."

"Is this why you guys have begged off going out to dinner with us the last few times?" Jake asked.

"Kinda, we tried to, for you, you know?" Craig glanced at the rear view and passenger side mirrors before switching lanes. "But I seriously can't with the wine swishing and sniffing—the endlessly boring discussion about the bouquet. Enough already… we get it… you're like a serious wine-dude but can we drink the shit already and move on to something else?"

"Wine-dude?"

"You know what I mean, and it would be one thing if I felt like he was genuinely excited about the wine, but it feels like he's a little more excited about showing off."

"He does get genuinely excited about the wine, but yeah, he also likes to show off a little. But that's not a horrible thing." Jake reached up, grabbing the bar above the window as Craig made another sharp turn. "We all know why every T-shirt you own is a size too small."

Jake pointed at Craig, whose face flushed, visibly embarrassed at being called out over his own vanity.

"You work out a lot and you look good," Jake said, without judgment. "You want people to see that. Victor has spent a great deal of time and money educating himself about wine and he likes to show that off."

"I guess you have a point, though I don't take off my shirt at the dinner table and give everyone a lap dance, that's all I'm saying."

"You should totally start!" Jake patted his lap. "Come on, you can practice on me."

Craig reached over and punched Jake in the arm. "Don't be a douche. You're like my brother."

"But from another mother so it's all good. Gyrate, baby, gyrate!"

"I'm telling my wife on you."

"She'll just laugh and think it's funny. Then she'll yell at you for telling me you both hate my boyfriend."

"We don't hate him, we just don't like him. Sophia *really* doesn't like him for you. Is it a money thing? He's able to keep you in the style to which you've become accustomed, growing up rich and all?"

"Wow, so I'm a materialistic gold digger, now? Thanks for that ringing endorsement."

"That came out wrong, you know I don't think you're a label queen."

"Where do you come up with this stuff? Label queen?"

He shrugged. "Don't pretend like it's not a thing."

Jake laughed, but decided not to comment further.

"We just want you to be happy, is all I'm sayin'."

"Preferably with someone you approve of, as opposed to my sugar daddy."

"Yeah, pretty much," Craig said, grinning like he was thrilled to have all that off his chest.

"Real nice."

"So exactly what's going on with the orgy guy?"

"What do you mean?" Jake asked. "And please stop referring to him as 'orgy guy', his name is Levi for fuck's sake."

"Touchy. You do realize that you're getting angrier about my dissing your non-friend than you did your boyfriend?"

"Can we not talk?" Jake asked.

"I know you, Jake, really well—"

"So that's a no on the whole non-talking idea?" Jake asked, cutting him off.

"—probably better than I'd like to admit," Craig continued, completely ignoring his pleas for silence, "so don't pretend as if you don't know what I'm talking about."

"I tried making a new friend, that's all. Seemed like I might have a lot in common with Levi." Jake turned, glancing out the passenger side window, afraid the disappointment over not having Levi be a part of his future might show on his face.

"Like the fact you wanna screw one another's brains out?"

Jake laughed. "I won't deny that I find him attractive, but I find you attractive and we've never screw—"

"Do *NOT* finish that sentence, I'm begging you."

"All I'm saying is I find a lot of men attractive but that doesn't mean I go out and have sex with them. I have a boyfriend who I've committed myself to. I've never broken that commitment." Jake decided that Craig seemed altogether unimpressed by that fact.

"Not that the same could be said for him," Craig muttered.

"It was one time," Jake said, wishing he'd never confided in Craig. "It was just sex. He slipped up. I wasn't going to throw our entire relationship away over one indiscretion."

"You're a bigger man that I am."

"And Levi… he's a really cool guy and I do like him, probably more than I should. If I were single, I'd ask him out, but I don't see why that fact should mean we can't be friends."

Craig shot him a sideways look. "Not sure my wife would agree if it were me and some other chick."

Jake frowned, but didn't offer any further justifications on the topic. For one, he didn't think he was doing anything wrong, even though somewhere deep down he suspected he might be potentially playing with fire, so perhaps not the smartest move ever?

All that being said, since Levi didn't want to be his friend, none of it fucking mattered.

Jake quickly shoved that thought aside, hoping that Levi would change his mind at some point down the road. Both he and Levi were grown-ups after all, and Jake knew he would never act on any feelings he may or may not have— which eventually would very likely pass anyway, as most of these things usually do when no one acts upon them. On top of that, he felt strongly that Levi wasn't the kind of man who would get romantically involved with someone who had a boyfriend, any more than he was the kind of boyfriend who would ever cheat on the side.

Knowing all of that to be true, Jake was confident a solid friendship could be forged out of all the chaos. He'd leave it alone for the time being and try again later. That little bit of hope, no matter how fruitless it may have seemed in reality, managed to lift his spirits.

He could feel Craig was still watching him so Jake flipped him off, smiling when his partner started laughing. He was still pissed at the man, but forced all that into the back of his mind. Jake was aware that Victor had changed over the years, hell they both had.

But that was to be expected, right?

They'd been together for nearly nine years. Victor had come into his life when Jake had felt more alone in the world than ever before. He'd lost his grandfather on his dad's side, who'd been Jake's favorite person in the entire world. Grandpa Frank had been Jake's one cheerleader. They never really talked much about the whole gay thing, but he'd said enough that Jake understood he wasn't going to lose him over it. His grandfather understood him in a way his father never could—Jake's yearning for a simpler, quieter life— they had that in common.

Jake hadn't truly felt whole since Grandpa Frank had passed away. Even his relationship with Julia had been strained at times. He was aware that she didn't understand him, but he knew she loved him as he did her.

His sister wanted him to be happy, and she didn't judge him for not wanting to be a part of the world their parents had created for them. She also wasn't ever going to defend him to their parents, which was fine. He understood that, even though it stung a bit for her to forever be the neutral ground on which he and his parents most often fought. Jake didn't want to be the cause of a rift in his sister's relationship with their parents, and he knew that her defending him to them would eventually do just that.

For a long time it had been him and Victor against the world—but there were times lately when it seemed like the world they were up against wasn't the same one. There'd been a gnawing fear deep in the recesses of his mind that he and Victor might want different futures—that they'd been in a holding pattern for several years, standing at a fork in the road, each waiting to see who was going to give in and compromise on the future they each wanted for themselves.

Jake had been at a loss for how to once again reunite those paths.

* * * *

Levi sat at his large, L-shaped desk watching the two-dimensional cubes on his screensaver bounce off the edges of his monitor and one another, mildly mesmerized and wondering if any of them would ever manage to break free, shooting off into cyber space, eventually popping up on some other computer screen in some other part of the world.

Today he felt like those cubes, trapped in a holding pattern, doomed to repeat the same thing over and over—no escape.

"You'll get a ton of work done that way," Valerie said from her desk located across the makeshift aisle they'd created with their desks.

"We should have totally had offices put in. We need more walls in this joint."

"You're the one who got all weird about not unnecessarily altering the original structure."

"In all honestly, that was just my nice way of not having to come out and say that I know you'd be napping all day if you had any amount of privacy."

"Yet here you are, zoning out—probably sleeping with your eyes open, you little freak."

Levi burst out laughing and chucked a pad of Post-Its at her head.

He missed unfortunately, which was made worse by the fact Valerie hadn't even attempted to duck, knowing he hadn't a chance in hell of hitting her. He went back to staring at his screen, deciding to ignore her snark. The truth was, they'd gotten a lot done since he'd come back from the coffee date from hell with Jake.

"That dude was totally into you." Valerie said.

"Who? Angelo?" Levi asked, wishing he actually gave a damn were that the case.

"Of course not!" He found the look of revulsion on her face amusing.

"Angelo was completely mesmerized by my beauty," Valerie added. "He's going to put a baby in me someday."

Levi's lip curled as that visual popped into his head and proceeded to make him nauseous. "Angelo is gay, lady, and don't pretend like you don't know it."

He laughed again when the Post-Its beaned him in the head, ricocheting off onto the floor at his feet.

"I was referring to the blue-eyed hottie who took you away and plied you with caffeinated beverages this morning."

"Ah!" Levi said with an overly dramatic sigh. "The guy with the boyfriend."

"Even better," Valerie said. "Love in the afternoon… with no attachments!"

"Ew, I can't be with him, I mean, ew! How tacky would that be? Cheap and tacky—some sort of holiday season affair? Nothing screams desperation like falling into *any* man's arms during this time of year."

"Sounds perfect—cheap equals hot," she said, fanning her vagina like it might be in danger of overheating. "Just what that tight little bum of yours desperately needs."

He cringed. "You're completely disgusting."

"Seriously, do you ever let that shit out to play or is it all forever encased in layers of sweaty, musky cotton, all shriveled and neglected?"

"That sorta talk certainly isn't going coax it outta hiding."

"You need to be kinder to your junk, punk."

"You just need to be kinder."

When she opened her mouth to utter further mind-numbingly hideous things Levi would never be able to purge from his already scarred and tortured brain, he held up a hand for her to stop. "Pretty please… go put together an estimate for the Freeman job."

"Well, all right, but only 'cause you're paying me to," she said, as if that were the only reason she might ever be helpful.

He glanced down at his crotch and pooched out his lower lip. "Sorry dude, but it's looking like nuthin' but sweaty, musky cotton for your foreseeable future."

"Are you talking to your crotch?" Valerie asked, watching him suspiciously.

"No!" Levi rolled his eyes acting as if she was completely insane for ever having suggested otherwise. "As if."

CHAPTER SEVEN

Spending his weekend in the country hadn't been on Levi's agenda, however, he'd realized a few weeks back that when working with Julia Freeman-Kingsley, agendas sometimes had to go the way of the wind. They'd looked at a half dozen other venues and had already reserved the Rainbow Palace, but apparently losing a massive deposit was of little to no consequence to the rich and famous. He'd been meaning to drive out and take a look at Glennellen for months and just hadn't had time due to his crazy schedule leading up to the cancer benefit.

The French-style chateau was constructed in 1926, for railroad tycoon Walt Whitney. Built entirely out of steel beam, concrete and stone, Glennellen had at one point, been one of the largest private residences in the country. Newly renovated and remodeled into a fifty-eight room luxury hotel, they had only just reopened their doors a few months before. Specifically geared toward hosting weddings and other lavish private events, the place was already booked out well into the New Year.

Julia had apparently placed her name on a cancellation list and called Levi excitedly when an opening came available for the weekend of her anniversary. Everyone had dropped everything in a mad dash to drive the three and half hours outside the city to take a look at the space. Julia had booked a small block of rooms, insisting they all spend the night. There was a wedding taking place that weekend, but Clare Mills, the catering and event manager for the hotel, assured Levi they would be able to see all the event space so long as they didn't mind working around the frenetic schedule of the wedding party.

Levi had bundled up and made the drive out to the estate early so he could introduce himself to Clare. Winter weather be damned, he wanted to make the most of the trip and walk through as much of the extensive gardens throughout the forty acre estate as he could handle. The property backed up to the Glenn Haven National park and wildlife preserve, which had once been the private hunting grounds for the uber-rich. Like most estates of its kind, Glennellen had switched hands multiple times throughout the years, eventually falling into total neglect and disrepair before being transformed into its current incarnation.

As he strode through the gardens, making his way back to the main building Levi couldn't help but notice how quiet and peaceful everything was. Gone were all the noises from the city—no sirens, garbage trucks or horns blaring. No angry screams from cabbies being cut off in traffic, no rattling from the commuter train as it rushed by from the tracks overhead—only the sound of the wind as it rushed by.

He'd snuck into the stables for a temporary respite from the cold and took time to pet the beautiful horses, but the cool air had quickly chilled him to the bone once again. In spite of the cold, Levi could picture how beautiful the property would look in the spring and summer, with the fountains gushing water up into the air, creating a fine mist to cool the skin. Gardens green and lush, heavily perfumed by the thousands of blooming flowers peppered throughout the grounds. Levi began to long for a winter no more, yearning to see all that he now imagined around him.

Within seconds, all of that faded away as Levi stopped in his tracks, looking upward and grinning as the snow started to fall.

"Cue the swelling romantic background music and enter the handsome stranger sent to sweep me off my feet stage right and I'd be starring in my very own movie."

As the snowflakes fell silently all around him, Levi sighed, marveling over the magical feeling he was currently swept up in as he started back toward the hotel once more. The clouds overhead made the warm glow from the lights along the arcade of Palladian windows stretching across the back of the hotel seem even more inviting. Lovely as the snow was, Levi was anxious for a large cappuccino to perk him back up and make him feel like a warm-blooded human again.

Before opening the thick wooden door that would take him back inside, he turned back and glanced over the grounds one last time. The ground was nearly snow covered now and Levi took one last mental snapshot to file away with the long list of potential themed events he would no doubt eventually plan at Glennellen.

* * * *

Heading back through the lobby toward the ornately carved, antique walnut check-in desk, he spotted Julia chatting with one of the desk clerks. He'd left his bags with the concierge desk since he'd arrived well before check in. As he approached she turned and waved.

"Yes, obviously I'm happy to pay for the room since we're cancelling last minute but my brother and his boyfriend were unable to join us after all."

"Ah, I see a note here in the comments noting that," the clerk said, tapping away on keyboard.

Levi tried to ignore his disappointment at not getting to see Jake this weekend, focusing instead on the silver lining—he wouldn't be subjected to watching Jake and Victor canoodling one another—assuming they were the type of couple who canoodled.

"Fortunately the wedding party here this weekend had a few last minute guests attending so there won't be any charge for canceling as the room won't go unused."

"Lovely, happy ending all around, then," Julia said, passing Levi a key card to his room. "We're all on different floors. Gregory and my parents are upstairs, settling in. Once you've done the same, let's meet up in the bar and we can go exploring from there."

Levi could sense she was really excited about the hotel and he glanced down at his watch. "It's nearly one now, so two?"

She nodded that was acceptable.

"I'll see if the events manager can meet us at two-thirty or three to show us the event space."

"Sounds perfect, Le…" she trailed off, staring over his shoulder at something behind him.

Her face went white so Levi turned to see what had spooked her. He could feel the blood draining from his own face watching Jake come to a slow, reticent halt a few feet away.

"Not exactly the response I was hoping for, sis," Jake said, cringing slightly.

Without saying a word, she turned and ran back to the reservation desk.

Jake dropped his bag on the ground at his feet. "I half expected you would be less than pleased to see me, but not Julia."

"I'm not unhappy to see you, Jake." Levi glanced back to see Julia's finger tapping on the counter impatiently. "She just canceled your room like five minutes ago."

"Oh." Jake began watching her as well. "I hadn't thought of that."

She turned and began walking back their direction shaking her head. "They already gave the room away."

"Gosh Julia, I'm sorry, I never thought about the room." Jake began chewing on his bottom lip—an act Levi was momentarily hypnotized by. "I found out last minute that my shift ended up getting covered so I haphazardly packed a bag and jumped in the car hoping to miss the snow."

"Where's Victor?" Julia asked, tapping her nail on her chin. "Wonder if there's any other hotels close by?"

"Vic had set up several conference calls when he thought we couldn't come, so he stayed behind." Jake bent over and picked up his bag. "I'll just go back home, it's not a big deal."

"No!" Julia said, frowning. "I'm thrilled you came, I just wish you'd called."

"Jake!" Gregory said, coming down the white marble staircase and rushing over to offer his brother-in-law a bro-hug. "So glad you made it after all."

"Thanks, Greg, really great seeing you as well, though it sounds like I'm homeless."

Greg looked at his wife who said, "It's a short and very tedious story, darling."

"I don't need to stay the night," Levi insisted, holding his key card out for Jake. "Once we've toured the facility, we can sit down and discuss how you'd like to proceed and I can take off after."

"I'm not taking your room," Jake said.

"Absolutely not, I want you to stay as well," Julia added. "We'll have loads to discuss tonight."

Jake hung the strap of his leather bag over his shoulder. "If I leave now, I can make it back to the city before the weather gets bad, but I won't have you driving at night in this, Levi."

"You're both staying." Gregory placed his arm around Julia. "I'm assuming Victor isn't with you since I don't see him anywhere. We've got a suite with a separate living room and Jake can take the sofa."

Jake cringed. "I hate imposing, Greg. You two get precious enough time alone as it is."

Julia stood up on her tippy toes and kissed her husband on the cheek. "It's all settled then."

"Sorry third-wheel, I made a vow to the little lady to always do everything within my power to give her anything her heart desires."

Levi could see Jake relenting, in spite of the smirk over the whole third-wheel insult. Julia was quite visibly set on this new plan and intent on getting her way.

Levi felt like a shit-heel for not offering to share his room with Jake, but Greg and Julia knew nothing about any of their… stuff. On top of that, he assumed his room was going to be small, somewhere back in what had once been the servant's quarters, or at least that was how he had interpreted Julia's 'being on different floors' comment. He wasn't sharing a tiny-ass bed with Jake, damn it—mainly because deep down he knew how badly he wanted to share his tiny-ass with the man instead, bed size be damned.

There was no way he trusted himself in that scenario.

* * * *

By the time Levi made it upstairs to his room, he felt even worse. For one, if his room had once been the servant's quarters, those were some posh, pampered housekeepers. The room was quite spacious, not a suite, but there was still a small living area with a TV, sofa and a small upholstered chair. The bed was massive, larger than his king-sized one back home and the bathroom was floor to ceiling marble with a huge, walk in shower.

There was an interesting mix of the new and old between the faded wall tapestries and antique sink faucets juxtaposed against the new carpeting and more modern furniture and flat-screen TV. The feature that really took his breath away was the two sets of French doors that led out onto a now snow-covered balcony which looked out across the back of the property. A thick, slate gray curtain hung on either side, allowing guests the ability to block out the light while sleeping.

Levi stood there, watching the snow fall before turning toward the bed, determined to do his best and let sleeping dogs lie, keeping his room to himself. It was all settled now anyway, so it would be weird if he brought it up again at this point.

He glanced down at his watch and saw that he only had about fifteen minutes left to himself. He grabbed his phone and made a quick call to check on Ruby, who informed him several times over how bad the weather was going to get. He could tell she was worried about it so he called Valerie after hanging up with his mother and asked if she would mind driving to Downham Parish and staying with Ruby overnight. They still didn't have a full-time nurse for her so they had been making do with several part-time nurses taking shifts. It was the best they could do at the moment, but it had ended up leaving gaps of time where no one was with her.

In truth, Levi could never fully relax when it came to Ruby. Though he knew it wasn't entirely true, it certainly felt as if there had always been this pressure on him to take care of her. He was the one man in her life who had always stuck by her—though Levi did sometimes wish that he didn't always have to be the parent in the relationship. It would be nice to have someone take care of him for a change. Not all the time, mind you, but to release the reins and allow someone else to chart a course now and again?

Levi could picture it in his mind's eye, but that was about as far as it went.

* * * *

They all stood in the lobby, saying their goodbyes to the event manager and Levi took a moment to pull Clare aside, thanking her for spending so much time with them. The Freeman clan was a tough crowd to please and it became evident to Levi early on that while Julia and Gregory loved Glennellen, the senator did not. What Harold didn't like, Gloria seemed destined to dislike as well and Jake had remained relatively silent throughout all of it.

It was odd, as Levi had never seen the man so quiet. Jake had made more noise during the friggin' movie they'd gone to see on their non-date, for Christ's sake. The one contribution Jake did finally make was recommending they all head into the bar for what Levi was expecting to be the unhappiest, Happy Hour ever.

"Well, I think we can all agree—" Harold began once they were all seated and had a cocktail in hand.

"It's beautiful!" Julia said excitedly. "I agree."

"Well, yes, it is that," Harold said.

Gloria placed a hand on Julia's arm. "It's a beautiful location, Julia, but I don't think it's fair to ask all our friends and family to make the three hour trek from the city for your anniversary party."

"That's why we book the entire place, Mother, so people can stay overnight."

Gloria smiled sweetly, though there was a hint of condescension in her tone. "Darling, I have a sinking suspicion that you've neglected to ask yourself one very important question."

Levi noticed Julia take her husband's hand under the table. "What would that be, Mother?"

"Do you really want to be stranded all the way out in the country inside the same building with your father's family?"

Jake snickered under his breath, quickly covering by pretending to cough. He and Gregory looked at one another knowingly and quickly took a drink.

Harold shot his wife one of his patented, less than pleased glares, which she completely ignored. That elicited the comment, "Yes, because your klepto-maniacal Aunt Tibby and that crackpot cousin, Millicent, who is so fond of sleeping with the hired help, are such a joy to have around."

Levi's eyes bugged out of his head slightly and he noticed Gloria's mouth open to respond with no-doubt equal venom only to smile at Levi and faux giggle instead.

"Every year we end up missing more of the silver and find ourselves needing to interview new staff," Harold muttered indignantly.

Family skeletons aside, Levi could see the place had been ruined for Julia and he felt bad for her. Jake was practically seething, visibly angry with Harold for speaking to his mother that way. Instead of offering comment, he leaned over and placed his arm around Julia's shoulder.

"It was a nice idea, though, huh?" Julia asked, rebounding like a well-seasoned pro when it came to handling disappointment.

"It was a grand idea, old girl," Jake said, grabbing his drink and clinking it gently against the one she'd left abandoned on the table in front of her. "They serve a damn fine cocktail, too."

She elbowed her twin gently in the gut and picked up her gin gimlet. Taking a sip, she nodded her head that the drinks were a bonus, indeed.

"We can come up some weekend just the two of us, babe," Gregory said, hoping that might further cheer her up.

Levi watched Gloria looking at her children and for the briefest moment he could see the sadness there, just behind her eyes, like it had been too long since she'd been able to see her babies as they were right now.

Thanks to some family background Levi had gotten from a late night conversation with Julia a few weeks back, Levi knew Gloria was equally culpable for Jake's self-inflicted banishment by not putting her foot down with her husband. That knowledge couldn't prevent Levi from feeling bad for her. He appreciated Ruby a little more in that moment. Even though there had been many times when he'd prayed his own mother would keep her opinions to herself, he never had to wonder whether or not his mother loved him.

He was fairly certain Jake wasn't likely to say the same about Gloria.

"That sounds fine, honey," Julia agreed, giving Gregory a polite peck on the lips.

In that moment, Levi decided that he simply had to ask Jake to share his room so Julia and Gregory could make the most of their evening at Glennellen. Looking at Gloria and Harold across the table, he decided that conversation could wait until they weren't around.

"Um, isn't that the guy from your office?" Jake asked.

Levi turned, completely shocked to see Angelo waving at him from the entryway between the bar and the lobby. Before he had time to react, Angelo started walking toward them. In the twenty seconds or so it took for Angelo to cross the bar and reach their table, Levi had just enough time to formulate an off-the-cuff and likely none-too-evil-genius plan.

"Apologies for the disruption, Julia," Levi said, standing and placing an arm around Angelo's waist. "This is my boyfriend…"

When Angelo began looking around in an attempt to see who Levi was referring to, he realized he should have given the evil-genius plan a little more time to percolate before pulling the trigger. Angelo's wide-eyed smile signified that he had finally worked things out, which is when he slid his arm around Levi's waist as well.

"Hi, honey." Angelo had a roguish smirk on his face that made Levi mildly nauseous. "Have some papers for you to sign."

A completely genius, brilliant rogue!

Julia was grinning and Levi knew the only thing that prevented her from pelting him with questions was the fact her parents were there.

"Will you all excuse us for a moment?" Levi asked, finally daring a glance at Jake only to see he was staring at Angelo, whom he didn't appear very happy to see.

"Of course, take your time," Julia insisted, smiling when Angelo winked at her.

Levi was dying inside, ready to kill himself and take Angelo down with him.

He whispered under his breath as he tugged none too gently on Angelo's arm. "You do not wink at Julia Freeman-Kingsley, Angelo—especially when her husband and her father, a United States Senator, are seated next to her."

"What's the big deal?" Angelo asked, looking adorably confused. "It didn't mean anything. I like dick. Your dick in particular, apparently."

"I am really, really sorry about that, Angelo. I don't know what I was thinking and I am completely mortified."

"Using me to make that Jake guy jealous is definitely working. Did you see the way he was looking at me?"

"That is not your business—"

"As your boyfriend, I beg to differ." Angelo winked at him.

Levi assumed that the whole winking thing must have charmed the pants off many conquests in the past, considering the man used them on nearly everyone.

"What the hell are you really doing here?"

"Valerie suggested I drive these up here to get them signed, something about a deadline and offering you some back-up? It wasn't a big deal, Levi. I was headed to my parents this weekend for a family thing. They live in Halton, it's like another hour up the interstate."

Levi took the documents from him, scanning the pages until he saw the deadline date, which was three weeks away and he rolled his eyes. Angelo seemed confused, looking over Levi's shoulder at the same date. He opened his mouth to no doubt voice that confusion but stopped himself, grinning like he was just now beginning to work out that he might be able to use this to his own advantage.

* * * *

Jake intently watched Levi and this Angelo asshole, failing miserably at attempting to read their lips. If they were boyfriends, it was either really new—like too new to be calling someone a boyfriend—or they had been dating for much longer and Levi was every bit as guilty for showing up at the theatre that night as Jake had been.

Funny Levi failed to mention that fact while he was attempting to persecute me by nailing me to the friggin' cheater wall.

Jake sucked down the rest of his bourbon, listening to the ice cubes clink as he set the glass back down on the table.

"I think your mother and I shall retire to our room before meeting you all for dinner," Harold said, following suit after Gloria stood.

"Your father will want a nap and I could use a freshening up."

"You've never looked lovelier my dear," Harold cooed.

Jake could feel his lip curling in disgust so he forced a smile in an attempt to keep the bile from rising any further. Sadly, he knew his parents well enough to understand his father was merely attempting to smooth over the feathers he'd ruffled when tossing Gloria under the bus by bringing up Aunt Tibby and Cousin Millicent.

Jake's smile became slightly more genuine for a moment, knowing she was going to lay into dear old dad over that one.

"We'll see you at dinner?" Gloria asked, lightly brushing the back of her hand across Jake's cheek. "You're looking a little pale, Jackson, I hope you're taking care of yourself."

Jake tried holding onto the gentle caress while doing his best to ignore the fact she'd referred to him by his given name, Jackson. Her touch said, *I love you* while the latter passive-aggressively screamed, *I still judge you for forsaking your birthright and cutting us out of your life all those years ago.*

"See you at dinner, Mother," Jake said, looking around for the waitress so he could order another drink.

He overheard his father asking her why she still bothered as his parents walked away. He turned to see Julia was watching him and he knew she'd heard it as well.

"You gotta try not to take that stuff personal, man," Gregory said, appearing to be a little disgusted by the exchange. "They can't see past their own view of the world."

"Whatever," Jake said, staring at Julia, who once again had nothing to say on the subject. "I stopped expecting them to ever come around years ago."

"I wish you wouldn't give up all hope," Julia said, appearing to be pissed at him. "The three of you always fighting and hating one another is very exhausting, Jake. I hate it and I hate feeling like the one thing you all have in common, everyone constantly looking to me expecting me to pick a side."

Jake's mouth fell open, ready to deny that fact until he realized he couldn't.

"I'm not ever going to do it, Jake. I love all three of you and none of you are ever going to make me choose one over the other."

"Okay, old girl," he said quietly, hoping his pet name for her might instill a shot of nostalgia into his tone.

She sighed, settling back into Gregory, her forehead all crinkled up in frustration. "I see the way they treat you and I know it's wrong. Daddy always wanted you to be just like him and the more he pushed the more you pushed back. And I say that knowing full well that you never wanted any of it, Jake. I'm not saying you should have made yourself miserable by going along with Daddy, but the way you reacted, cutting them completely off, refusing to see them or talk to them— that wasn't right either. Believe it or not, you completely crushed Mother. She was devastated and the two of them bickered constantly for over a year because of it."

Jake could feel himself getting angry, knowing full well that he was the last person who could be objective on the topic. "I have never asked you to intervene on my behalf, Julia, and, I never will. I never wanted to hurt them."

"I know that, Jake," Julia said. "I get it, I do. It's all very frustrating."

"I reached a point where I simply couldn't have the same argument with them any longer." He caught the cocktail waitress's attention and lifted his glass in the air, signaling they needed another round. "I couldn't keep going back, hoping things would get better or expecting a different outcome. It was killing me, turning me into someone I didn't recognize. You always wanted what they wanted for you, so you never had to work hard in order to please them."

He could see that her eyes had begun to well up, so he reached over and took her hand.

"Just promise me that you and I will start spending more time together, baby brother," Julia said.

"I can do that, old girl," Jake said.

Julia turned and looked back out at Levi. "Something seems off about that."

Jake and Gregory started laughing.

"I didn't mean it like that." She shrugged, thanking the waitress for dropping off the drinks. "I knew he met someone a few weeks ago. He was practically glowing the day we had that first meeting with Mom and Dad."

"Well there's your proof, darling," Gregory said, visibly confused.

"He's certainly attractive, don't get me wrong," Julia said. "Admittedly, I don't know all that much about Levi, though I like to think of him as a friend. I don't know, I just don't picture that guy as the type for Levi."

"I know he works for Levi," Jake said, taking a drink before turning to see Julia and Gregory staring back at him wide-eyed. "I saw the guy at his office." They each sat up in their seat a little which made Jake feel like sinking back into his. "We met for coffee… once. We're friends… sorta."

"How does one become *sorta* friends?" Julia asked.

Gregory sat back again, a pained expression on his face like Jake had just gotten himself busted.

"No!" Jake insisted. "There's nothing hinky going on between us, jeez. You know we met because of his mother."

"I'm sorry." Julia still looked perplexed. "You show up here without Victor. Combine that with the fact *you* are exactly the type of guy that I could see Levi falling for, that the two of you are *sorta* friends and Levi's new beau looks like a gigolo he's hired in a desperate attempt to make you jealous, and it's no wonder my mind started to wander."

"Alrighty then," Gregory reached across the table and took Julia's drink away from her.

"Oh sure, make like I'm the crazy one," she said, frowning.

"You said it, sister," Jake said, as the three of them all began to laugh.

* * * *

"Wipe that cocky grin right off your face, Angelo," Levi said, glancing back toward the bar to see Harold and Gloria heading up the stairs toward their room located on the second level. "Do not utter a single friggin' word, so help me."

"As your boyfriend, I have certain needs."

Levi started laughing, completely mortified that he had looked both Jake and Julia in the face and flat out lied about he and Angelo being a couple. It was silly.

"The best thing about me, babe, is that I always make sure I'm meeting all your needs while in pursuit of my own."

"You can stop now," Levi said, "you're my faux-boyfriend, so any sex we have will be imaginary as well."

Angelo frowned. "This relationship isn't working for me."

He could tell Angelo was fully enjoying the teasing-torture he was inflicting upon Levi. "Well, you do work for me, and as humiliated as I feel for unwittingly dragging you into the insanity that is my personal life, let's try not to confuse and muddle things up any more than they already are."

"I'll do my best, but I make no promises because the more you resist me, the more I find myself wanting to have you."

Levi fanned his face, feeling himself begin to blush— something Angelo seemed pleased to see. "You're a very bad man."

"Your friend is headed this way."

"The guy?" Levi asked, feeling his panic-sweat kick into high gear. "The Jake?"

Angelo cocked an eyebrow. "So that *is* what's going on here."

"Shut up, kiss me like you mean it… and then pretty please, go back to your car and drive *safely* to your parents' house. Then I can call Valerie and tell her she's dead to me."

Angelo laughed under his breath before taking Levi into his arms and planting a searingly hot kiss upon his lips.

Levi was completely caught off-guard when Angelo thrust his tongue into his mouth, realizing that he and Angelo had different ideas about 'kissing like you mean it'. For Levi, it meant in a 'love and cherish me' sort of way— for Angelo it apparently meant 'porno tongue'.

Both fearing and hoping Jake was watching, Levi decided to roll with it, kissing Angelo back while hoping all the other complete strangers in the lobby didn't think he was trashy. The instant his cock began to react favorably to the new stimuli, Levi jerked away, attempting to regain his composure as he gently patted Angelo on the cheek.

His face-patting got a little harder once the smirk of satisfaction made an appearance.

"You can go now, *honey*," Levi growled under his breath.

Angelo laughed as he turned, making his way through the lobby toward the entrance.

"That was some kiss," Jake said from behind him.

Levi took a few seconds to compose himself before turning to face him. He tried not to wince as that old familiar pain shot through his chest the instant Jake met his gaze.

"Angelo's a passionate guy," Levi said, smiling weakly. "In the short time we've been dating I've figured out it's easier to go with his flow since he doesn't seem to be capable of dialing things back to my pace."

Jake folded his arms across his chest, something Levi had begun to realize was a defense mechanism he utilized when confronted with something that he found uncomfortable—like the time their hands had touched during their movie date or the time he met Jake's afore unmentioned boyfriend in Julia's apartment.

"You seem irritated by something?" Levi asked.

An incredulous expression came across his face as Jake shrugged. "Nope. Nothing bothering me."

Levi could see that Julia was watching the two of them from her perch in the darkened, wood paneled lounge of the bar.

"Great. Good," Levi said. "Because I'm gonna suggest something that I hope you'll please not take the wrong way. I think it would be nice for Julia and Gregory to have some alone time. She was pretty disappointed when confronted with the realization that this place wasn't going to work for her party."

"Because deep down, she'd like for *her* anniversary to be more than a political device for my evil, imperialistic father," Jake said, the tone in his voice getting all dark and angry sounding.

Hello, Daddy issues.

Levi decided to steer clear of that particular land mine. "Maybe a romantic evening alone in their own room…"

Jake grinned in a way that made Levi believe he might attempt to twist this into something untoward.

"You wanna share your room with me?"

"The bed is enormous, though if that feels problematic, I'd be happy to crash on the sofa, it looked pretty comfy." Levi glanced back into the bar at Julia who was all snuggled against her husband, both seated in an oversized leather chair next to the fireplace. Greg's arm was around her shoulder and they looked adorable, relaxed, not worried about being watched or photographed.

"They look sweet, huh?" Jake asked, throwing his arm around Levi's shoulders while letting out a long, melodramatic sigh. "*Please* tell me we're gonna talk about boys and braid one another's hair?"

"I'm already sorry I brought it up."

"Is there a fireplace?" Jake asked excitedly, as Levi shrugged his arm off. "We can roast marshmallows and tell ghost stories!"

"You are totally weird, dude," Levi said.

"What? I never had many sleepovers as a kid."

"They have a five-star, award winning chef running all things culinary in this Gin Joint. I seriously doubt they have marshmallows lying around."

"Well, this place sucks."

Levi rolled his eyes, laughing when Jake shoved him playfully.

In truth, Levi never had many sleepovers when he was a child either, for obvious reasons. Most of the other moms didn't trust Ruby to watch over their children, for one. Beyond that, Levi had also been a bit of a loner as a child, suddenly realizing that things hadn't changed all that much over the years. In truth, he was more nervous about being alone in room all night with Jake than anything else.

"I wonder if they have any board games in the hotel?" Jake asked, pretty much talking to himself at this point.

"Something tells me after a long dinner with your parents, you'll no longer be in the mood to play games."

"You're a cold, cruel man, Levi Goode." Jake peered in toward the bar. "I should buy a bottle of brandy now to soothe the wounds that will no doubt be inflicted by my father's forked tongue later."

"Um, yeah… No hooch in the hotel room," Levi said, able to imagine the atrocities the two of them would be likely to commit against one another locked in a hotel room with a bottle of brandy.

Jake appeared genuinely stung by the no-hooch rule, glaring at Levi like he'd just taken his favorite coping mechanism away. Then, the *why* dawned on him and he cleared his throat, visibly uncomfortable all of a sudden.

"Right then, no hooch it shall be." He pointed into the bar. "We should go tell the happy couple?"

"After you, Captain Renault," Levi said, motioning with his hand for Jake to go first.

"Please," Jake said, looking shocked over the Casablanca reference. "You're Mr. Anti-Hooch, pal. If one of us is the Louis in this relationship, it's gonna be you."

Levi laughed, following Jake back into the bar feeling a little less anxious about the new room assignments. They both had boyfriends now, well, Jake thought so at any rate, which placed an added layer of self-professed security over the situation.

One dinner and one night of self-restraint and he'd be back home, safe and sound and breaking up with his new faux-boyfriend.

Between Valerie and my own questionable, desperation-inspired behavior, it'll be a miracle if I don't get slapped with a sexual harassment suit before it's all said and done.

* * * *

"Oh my God," Jake said, falling backward onto the bed, his face pale and his arms folded across his stomach, like he might be ill at any moment. "I feel shorter."

Levi laughed, heading for the mini-fridge.

"Do I look shorter?" Jake asked. "I totally *feel* shorter."

"No, don't be silly," Levi said, lying through his teeth. "You're every bit the tall drink of water you were before heading down to dinner."

"I don't believe you," Jake said, frowning. "But please continue with more ego strokage."

He felt bad for Jake, having sat through an entire meal being passive-aggressively jabbed with barb after barb by the senator who was not-so-good to his own flesh and blood. He wanted to hug the man, but figured a mini bottle of liquor would be safer.

"There is no stroking allowed," Levi said. "New rule."

Jake looked up, staring warily at the tiny bottle Levi was holding out for him.

"What happened to the no-hooch rule?" he asked.

"After the night you've had, I can't think of anyone who deserves to toss back a few more." Levi wiggled the bottle at him. "Go on, Jake, seriously."

Jake sat up and took the bottle from him. "So you picked up on it too?"

"I'd have to be a pretty big fucking moron not to." Levi removed his jacket and tossed it over the back of a chair. "Never in all my life, have I heard that many back-handed compliments thrown about in such a short amount of time."

"Thank you!" Jake fought for a moment, straining to get the tiny twist top off the bottle. "Vic always claims that I'm just imagining it."

Levi scowled, realizing he'd just inadvertently called Jake's boyfriend a fucking moron.

His discomfort was quickly replaced with shame-inducing glee over the fact Victor was turning out to be such a douche. The glee was short lived, however, realizing he was losing out on a totally great guy to a moronic douche.

"Well, perhaps Victor is right," Levi offered, "he's spent more time around them than I have."

"Don't do that." Jake turned the bottle upside down and sucked down every last drop. "I need more people on my side. My father is the devil and my mom once again sat idly by, saying nothing."

"Julia was there, though, and she and Gregory helped considerably by continually changing the subject."

"As did you," Jake said, this pleady, grateful expression taking over his face. "I wanted to kiss you for picking up on things and jumping in to help keep the conversation steered away from me as much as you did."

"Kissing is also not allowed in the room," Levi said, smirking when Jake scowled at him.

Levi felt bad for him, knowing full well he would still be lying on the dining room floor, completely reduced to a puddle if the shoes had been on the other feet. He was suddenly happier about the fact he would never know who his own father was. After witnessing Harold's behavior it seemed like it might be a blessing.

Jake's shoulders still appeared slouched over as he stared into the carpet like it was a crystal ball he hoped might offer answers to life's greatest mysteries.

"I think you're probably gonna need one more of those," Levi nudged his head toward the empty bottle Jake was still clutching desperately in his hand. "I'm gonna hop in the shower," Levi said, pointing to the bathroom.

"You feel dirty, no doubt," Jake said wide-eyed. "I need a fucking *Silkwood* bath after that dinner."

Levi laughed at the imagery, grabbing a pair of briefs and an undershirt from his bag. He hadn't packed any sort of lounge wear or pajamas, intending to free-ball it as he hadn't planned on sharing a room. Luckily he always brought along extra pairs of underwear and socks when he traveled—something Ruby had always insisted he do whenever they vacationed as a child. He wasn't quite sure why to this day, but he still did it, as if traveling without them would be bad luck.

"Silly superstitions," he muttered.

* * * *

Turning off the shower, Levi felt like a whole new man after being pelted by hot pulsating bursts of water from nearly every direction. Despite having not initially been a huge fan of the dark, pinkish-brown floor-to-ceiling marble in the bathroom, were it possible to fold this particular shower stall up and take it home with him, he totally would.

"I would fucking marry this shower I love it so much," he said, lifting the chrome metal latch and pulling on the heavy glass door.

His head cocked to the side, confused when the door didn't open. He shook his head and tried pushing on the door instead, more confused when it still didn't budge. A closer inspection of the latch revealed the screw had come loose, so when he lifted the latch handle on the inside of the door, the other end on the outside didn't move along with it. Since the door apparently only opened inward, he was trapped.

He stood there, completely naked and dripping wet, staring at the confounded thing for a moment, trying to work out how he might go about getting himself out of this mess. Jiggling the door didn't seem to help, and he was afraid he might break the glass if he yanked on it too hard. While there was a slit-like opening between the two larger panels of glass, he hadn't had the foresight to bring a credit card into the shower with him, and a quick inspection of the things he had brought revealed none of it would be useful in this particular instance.

Cursing under his breath, Levi realized he was stuck and left with only one option—call Jake for help.

"Which is awesome since I'm completely naked," he said sarcastically.

The only saving grace in that moment was thinking about the pickle he'd be in were Jake *not* staying in the hotel room with him. He'd be trapped until housekeeping found him the next day.

That thought sent a wave of panic through him.

"Jake!" he yelled out, beginning to shiver as the temperature of the room cooled.

It took several more screaming pleas for help before he got any response.

Levi strained to make out the words hearing Jake finally yelling something through the door.

"I'm stuck!"

He waited a few seconds, finally seeing the door crack open.

"Who the hell is Chuck?" Jake asked.

Levi rolled his eyes. "Stuck, damn it, I'm stuck in this stupid shower."

Jake poked his head in the bathroom and Levi's hands instinctively went straight over his crotch, covering his bits and baubles. He removed one just long enough to point at the latch.

"Can you please let me out?"

Jake pushed open the door and entered the bathroom. The closer he got to the shower door the wider his smile became. He finally reached the door, placing a hand on the outer latch, then stood there as if inventorying every last inch of Levi's naked body through the glass.

"Dude," Levi said, causing Jake to jump slightly.

"Sorry, my bad." Jake lifted the latch and pushed open the door.

Levi stood there, hands covering his junk as Jake once again took a nice long look, as if hypnotized by the sight of wet skin and muscle.

"Kinda freezing here," Levi said, completely mortified or more likely terrified he might sprout a boner any second if Jake continued to eye-fuck him too much longer.

"*God*, sorry… again." Jake spun around and made a beeline out of the bathroom, pulling the door closed behind him.

"Well, that wasn't weird!" Levi yelled, scrambling for a towel.

"Sorry!" He heard Jake scream back from the bedroom, better able to hear since the door hadn't quite closed all the way.

"It's… fine," Levi said, wrapping a towel around his waist and opening the bathroom door before stepping into the bedroom. "I got a little stressed when I couldn't get out, that's all."

Jake had taken his shirt off and was rummaging around through his bag. "So you're claustrophobic?"

"Sure." Levi spun right back around and closed the door, deciding he needed to mentally prepare himself before seeing Jake in the buff.

God, I'll have to let him out of the shower.

He shook that image out of his head, deciding to brush his teeth.

Jake pushed the door back open, walking in wearing nothing but his briefs.

"I'm assuming we can we dispense with the formalities since I've pretty much seen you naked?"

"Um… I guess?" Levi mumbled over the toothbrush shoved in his mouth.

"Awesome." Jake stepped over to the shower and turned the water on.

Levi looked up at the ceiling when Jake yanked his briefs down. He bent over and spit, deciding now was a great time to vacate.

"Can you latch the door closed?"

"Just leave it cracked."

"Come on, water is getting everywhere," Jake said. "I don't have anything you've never seen before."

Levi walked over to the shower and latched the door. He noticed Jake was not bothering to cover his own bits and baubles, but Levi kept his eyes planted firmly on the man's face nonetheless.

Jake started laughing, no doubt seeing that Levi wasn't going to ogle him like a piece of meat, the way Jake had him. He wanted to do that, but his desire to deprive Jake of the satisfaction won out.

He sneered. "You're a much stronger man than I am, okay. Happy now?"

"I've always suspected as much," Levi said, smugly, before turning to leave. "Lemme know when you're ready to get out."

He rounded the corner and headed straight for the mini fridge where he snagged a tiny bottle of vodka. He caught a glimpse of his reflection in a mirror hanging on the wall and could see his own judgment staring back at him.

"Jake got one? *Two!* Jake got two teeny bottles." Levi said, pointing at himself and deciding that was all the justification he needed. He opened the bottle and sucked it down, hissing from the alcohol burn.

"This is definitely one of those instances when not having had sex for..." he paused, counting back the months, his mouth falling open when he realized how long it had actually been. "Christ, no wonder I'm such a basket case!"

"What?" Jake called out from the bathroom.

"Nothing!" Levi yelled back. He'd intended to rub one out in the shower, but he felt weird doing that when he knew Jake would likely be using it right after him.

He decided to get dressed then realized he left his briefs and T-shirt in the bathroom. He glanced back at his reflection and asked. "You did that on purpose didn't you?"

* * * *

Levi stretched out across the bed trying to keep his eyes focused on the ceiling instead of sneaking peeks at a towel-clad Jake as he moved about the room.

Eyes on the ceiling, Scumbalina, that is someone else's man and you don't need to be coveting what you're never going to have.

Levi 'accidentally' took another look.

Holy fuck he is smokin' hot. I wanna lick all of that and… Gah! I said don't think about it! Do not covet, asshole! And stop thinking about assholes. Christ!

In that moment, he understood Jake's shower gawking and felt a twinge of guilt over giving him such a hard time. He wondered if Jake had been thinking similar types of things about him. He couldn't manage to think of a more dangerous rabbit hole to fall into, so Levi did his best to purge the entire line of inquiry before his brain imploded.

Feeling bad had never felt so good and Levi hated that. He was going to make it through this night by keeping his dirty, wanton lusting to himself and then spend the rest of his life avoiding Jake Freeman at all costs. There was no way Levi could be this man's friend. It would never freakin' work. He wanted so much more from a relationship with Jake, and there might have been a chance that the two of them could co-exist within the same world, were it not for the glaringly obvious fact that Jake was also every bit as into him.

One-sided lust was potentially doable if not altogether painful for the poor sap left out in the cold, but two-sided lust would lead to nothing but trouble. One slip-up would lead to the most awesome sex ever, quickly followed by drama and screaming and pointy-fingered accusations. Reputations had been eviscerated over this sort of thing since the beginning of time and Levi wasn't willing to sacrifice his career for a few precious moments of undoubtedly satisfying, hot, totally hard… bliss.

"Penny for your thoughts?" Jake asked, pulling on a pair of boxer briefs under his towel.

Levi shook his head, turning away. He spotted Jake's iPod lying on the bed, earbuds haphazardly tossed across the thick embroidered duvet cover, realizing why it had taken Jake so long to hear him screaming for help. He reached over and snagged it, placing a bud in one ear while looking at Jake suspiciously.

"Let's see what we have here."

Jake grinned, yanking the towel free before walking it back to the bathroom and tossing it onto the floor.

Levi tapped the screen, pressing play and the falsetto harmonies of old school funky rock blared into his ear. Levi quickly turned the volume down.

"My God, you're like deaf," he said, tapping the 'Now Playing' link in order to see who the singer was. "Who loves you pretty momma?" he asked, repeating the lyrics. "Who the hell are the Four Seasons, grandpa?"

Jake sneered, not appreciating the added color commentary. "I can't believe you don't know who the Four Seasons are."

"Simmer down there, indignator." Levi shrugged. "Never been much of a music guy."

"It hurts my soul to hear you say that." Jake flopped down next to Levi on the bed and placed the other ear bud into his ear as the next song started to play.

"Oh, I've heard this one!"

Jake smiled over Levi's excitement.

"Don't judge me," Levi said, sarcastically, "your soul is apparently in jeopardy here."

Jake sung along in a screeching falsetto that had Levi's eyes bugging out of his head.

"Wow!" Levi scooched back across the bed a little. "Did the windows just crack?"

Jake busted out laughing, rolling onto his back and placing his hands over his belly.

"Seriously though, what's up with the doo-wop, dude?"

"I *love* this music," Jake said, once he managed to stop laughing. "There's something magical that happens whenever I listen to Frankie Valli. It's like, no matter how shitty my day has been, these songs make me feel better. A couple of tunes in and I'm smiling and dancing—"

"And singing?" Levi asked. "Assuming that's what we're calling what just happened here."

Jake smacked him in the arm. "Don't be an asshole, Goode."

"So it's your Prozac?"

Jake nodded, visibly liking the sound of that.

"Alrighty then." Levi laid back and listened along. He started tapping his foot and bobbing his head back and forth. He was just getting ready to give these Four Seasons dudes his personal seal of approval when the ear bud was ripped from his ear.

"I will not be disparaged," Jake insisted, apparently attributing Levi's head bobbing to be sarcasm.

"Sheesh, man, I was just going to say that I liked it." Levi rubbed his ear. "You cracker."

Jake eyed him suspiciously for a moment, then relented, offering him the bud back. "Sorry."

They both settled back onto the bed and just listened for a few minutes, occasionally looking at one another.

"It's a little odd that the child of *the* Vegas showgirl of the eighties doesn't like music," Jake said.

"No, I never said I didn't like music, just that I'm not a 'music guy'," he said, using air quotes. "I like music just fine but I'm typically okay listening to whatever happens to be on the radio."

Jake was staring at him like he was an alien.

"Don't judge me."

"Too late," Jake said, smirking at him. "I'll admit that my taste in music comes from my grandfather, my dad's dad. Growing up, we'd visit the farm in the summers, Grandpa Frank and I would spend hours listening to all his old vinyl. There was an entire wall of shelves in his den that housed all his LPs. He actually left them all to me when he passed away."

"When did he die?" Levi asked.

Jake didn't answer for a moment, staring off into space, lost in his own thoughts or memories. Levi found it difficult to catch his breath all of a sudden, staring at what had to be the single best looking man he had ever seen, all stretched out across the bed.

"Long time ago, back when I was in college." Jake finally answered, ripping Levi out of his obsessing. "He loved music, you know, all of it—jazz, rock and roll, classical, hell even disco. But Frankie Valli and The Four Seasons were his favorite—they were innovators."

Levi nodded, though in truth he had no clue what the man was going on about.

"Guess that's part of what makes these particular songs special to me. I can close my eyes and go back there again, with him, you know? Hot summer nights, with the windows open and the cicadas singing through the trees, drinking cold Coca Cola and dancing around the den to these songs with Julia, making our grandparents laugh."

That part Levi could totally understand. "You miss him."

"Every day," Jake said. "He was the only person in my family who got me."

Levi tentatively reached across the bed, squeezing Jake's hand, letting him hang on a little longer than intended when Jake refused to let go of him.

"What's with you and your mom?" Jake asked. "She's such a trip. I'd imagine growing up with Ruby would have been a blast."

Levi shook his head. "Everyone always says how much they admire her free spirit."

Jake chuckled under his breath, rolling onto his side, facing Levi. "I'm assuming her free spirit wasn't fun for you?"

"When I was really little, I loved it. Ruby was like a fabulous cartoon character. Every day was some new game, for which there were no rules. But the older I got, the more I began to long for a few rules. There was always a new guy and we moved around a lot. The same city, mind you, just different apartments. Sometimes we lived in mobile homes off Tropicana Blvd, depending upon where Ruby happened to be working at the time and how much money she was or wasn't making. I remember at some point, thinking that life with Ruby was like living on quicksand." Levi turned his head to look at Jake. "Nothing was permanent except for me and her—my one and only constant."

"So you had to grow up really fast."

Levi nodded. "Something like that. Then she got sick and I got terrified."

"You thought you were going to lose your one and only constant." Jake nodded, signaling that he understood. "What she had, pneumonia with sepsis, it's nasty stuff and with the added complications of heart failure—a whole lot of people die from that every year, Levi."

"For days I sat in the waiting room of that hospital as a revolving door of her dancer friends and a plethora of exes came and went."

"I can't believe no one from the hospital noticed you were alone all that time and called someone to be with you."

"Oh, I left often enough, leaving at night when one of her girlfriends did, so it looked like I wasn't on my own, and then waiting in the main lobby the next morning until I spotted another of her friends coming into the hospital who I could follow back up."

"That's the saddest thing I've ever heard, Levi."

"I learned very early on that there was no one I could count on, but me. Things were better after we relocated here. Money was tighter, as Ruby couldn't manage to hold onto a job for very long—she either got fired due to that free spirit of hers or because she fell ill too often. That's how she eventually ended up on disability."

"I guess what I appreciated about your mother is that she always says what she means. So different than the home that I grew up in, where no one said what they meant."

"I can see that." Levi smiled.

"It's so odd to me that no one has taken you off the market before now," Jake said, propping himself up with a pillow he snagged from the top of the bed. "I think you're so great, as you well know by now."

"I work a lot, and that tends to squash any time for meeting people."

"That why you started dating Angelo?"

"You mean, 'cause he works for me?"

Jake nodded, trying to hold back the snarky grin and failing miserably.

He decided not to answer, which seemed the safest bet since he wasn't actually dating Angelo for real.

"What about you and Victor?" Levi asked. "What made you fall for him?"

"He had a massive ego, which I mistakenly took for confidence." Jake smirked when Levi laughed. "Two totally different things, but also, he listened to all my sad stories and never judged me, which was refreshing."

"I kinda did that, huh?"

"You were angry and you lashed out, Levi. Considering I wasn't completely honest with you, well-meaning motives or not, I kinda led you on, so you had good reason to be pissed."

"I guess."

"Allow me to apologize for my parents, by the way. That dinner… so humiliating. Growing up, I felt like a tool trotted out during election years to obtain votes for my father, who pretended to love his gay son, all the while telling me what a disappointment I was."

"Why do they disapprove of what you do so much? I think it's a really noble thing, being a paramedic… seeing people in the absolute worst moments of their lives?"

"Because being a paramedic isn't special enough for a Freeman, naturally." Jake sighed. "Saving lives wasn't okay unless I was going to go to medical school and become a doctor. All Harold cared about was how it would look to voters. Of course the son of a bitch wasn't above using my career path during his campaign to try and connect with the 'working man' voter."

Levi cringed, completely able to understand why that would piss Jake off.

"I finally had to threaten him in order to get him to stop pimping me out like he was proud of who I was, when nothing could be further from the truth."

"Let me guess, that's when your relationship went south?"

"Yep, nail on the head there, buddy. That was a few months after I'd met Victor. I was convinced he'd break up with me once he found out that connection with my parents had been permanently severed. He knew the relationship was strained, because he'd asked a lot of questions when we first met."

"Well, yeah, but that's kinda natural when you first start dating someone."

Jake shook his head. "Totally normal, but growing up in the public eye makes you paranoid and suspicious of strangers. So often people only tried getting close to me because they thought they could get something out of it. And in my experience, too many personal questions were usually a sign that a guy liked the idea of my family more than they liked me."

"That just seems crazy to me, Jake, you're..." Levi trailed off, realizing he was about to say too much. "...neat."

"Um... don't strain yourself trying to come up with an adequate adjective or anything."

Levi shot him a nasty look. "You were saying what about your *boyfriend?*"

Jake sneered at Levi. "That it turned out Victor didn't care about my family after all. He has always been extremely motivated—determined to make a success of himself or die trying. If I were a daughter, Victor would have been exactly the type of man my father would have wanted for a son-in-law. He grew up poor, worked hard, studied hard, and got accepted into an Ivy League school on a full scholarship.

Victor is a self-made man—a fantastic back story that would've played well to the masses were it not for the fact he was playing hide the sausage with me." Jake laughed under his breath, as if suddenly realizing he was getting worked up. "Shit, I'm sorry, Levi. You can't possibly want to hear about this stuff."

"It's cool."

Jake cringed, and Levi could tell he'd done a sucky job selling it.

"Guess the moral of our combined stories is that you and I have unhappy childhoods in common."

"Lucky us," Levi said sarcastically.

"Being with Victor, that was never a money thing for me, though."

Levi was surprised by that statement. "Did I ever give you the impression I thought otherwise?"

"No, of course not, another friend mentioned it to me a few weeks back. Guess I'm a little sensitive about it."

"Does that mean there's some truth to it?" Levi asked, laughing when that panicked expression came back over Jake's face.

"Stop fucking with me, asshole," Jake said.

"I'm cold." Levi shivered slightly. "Think I'm getting under the covers."

He removed the ear bud and handed it to Jake, who turned the music off and placed the iPod on the nightstand. Levi could feel Jake's eyes on him as he slipped off his T-shirt and slid under the covers.

Levi watched as Jake got into bed. "Sorry if I pried too much with all the questions."

Jake laughed, pretending like he could barely see Levi across the wide expanse of mattress between them.

"This bed is massive."

Levi scooted a little closer to the center as did Jake.

"Perfect for the couple who wants to ensure they never have to touch one another," Jake said, using a game show host voice as if he were attempting to use that as a selling feature.

Levi laughed, feeling bad that he was so willing to throw in the towel on a potential friendship with Jake. How short-sighted could he be? They were from totally different backgrounds, yet despite that, they had a lot in common.

As if he'd been able to read his thoughts, Jake said, "So does all the nudity and personal tragedy stories mean that we're going to try being friends, now?"

"I suppose," Levi said nonchalantly.

"Well, try to contain your excitement, Levi, sheesh."

Levi let out a belly laugh, placing a hand over his tummy.

"I really want you in my life, you jerk, so try and pretend as if you're excited about that as well."

"Okay." Levi cleared his throat and did a fist pump into the air. "Friends… yeah!"

Jake smiled. "That was pathetic."

"Hey, I'm still shocked I'm rewarding your crummy behavior by becoming friends with you."

Jake rolled over onto his side, facing Levi. "Thank you for overlooking my shortcomings."

"The will be no coming, short or otherwise," Levi said, rolling onto his side, facing Jake. "That's rule number one for this new friendship."

"There's rules for our friendship already? We just became friends like one minute ago!"

"Well, you and I are going to be friends with conditions."

"Hmm... That sounds less fun than friends with benefits."

"Will you please be serious?"

"What, I'm excited, damn it, I have a new best bud."

Levi scoffed. "Whoa... best buds? I think you're jumping the gun there, pal."

Jake started snickering, trying to keep himself from laughing out loud over Levi's gullibility.

"Un-puff your ego, Freeman."

"How dare you!" Jake said, pretending to be shocked. "I am not puffy."

"We should go to sleep while we're ahead." Levi rolled over, dramatically rustling the covers and punching his pillow as he resituated himself.

"Lemme guess, night terrors?" Jake asked, snickering when no response came from the other side of the bed. "Dude, that was funny with all the pillow punching and whatnot."

"There's nothing in *my* bed that frightens me," Levi finally said, smiling to himself.

"Yikes. So the new boyfriend's got a teeny-weenie then, huh?"

"Oh my God, could you be any more inappropriate?"

"Is that a serious question?" Jake asked.

"No!" Levi insisted. "God, no."

"You just seem like... I mean... I just assumed you were a bottom, so..." He trailed off, watching Levi turn back over out of the corner of his eye.

"We are so not talking about sex."

"No sex talk? Like ever?"

"That's right."

"But friends are supposed to talk about sex," Jake reminded him.

"Yet this feels more like an interview tactic."

"You're a very suspicious individual."

"Of course, it would be *my* problem."

"You have issues talking about sex, I understand, no judgment."

"I don't have iss—" Levi stopped mid-sentence and took a deep breath. "I love talking about sex, okay? I would totally talk about nothing else if I could, but—"

"Awesome, I'm a top, though I can be versatile, however I don't really enjoy getting fucked all that much. It's okay, you know, just not my preference."

Levi sat up in the bed. "*Major* over-share."

"What? You just said—"

"You didn't let me finish!"

"If you're ashamed about being a bottom, that's okay Levi. I know some guys have issues admitting that they enjoy getting fucked. It goes back to those silly gender roles, all that man's-gotta-be-a-man BS. But I've always thought it took more bravery to allow another man inside me, you know?"

"OMG, please stop talking."

"Dude, I'm your friend now, and friends don't judge."

"Said the man judging me for being the type of guy who won't admit to being a bottom."

"So you are a bottom," Jake said excitedly, before settling back down.

"I am a bottom," Levi said, longing for another mini bottle of vodka. "A great big cock whore from *way* back."

"That's cool," Jake said, as if he'd not just made a huge ordeal about getting this information from Levi.

"Can we go to sleep now?" Levi asked.

"Sure, totally."

Levi scooched across the bed and turned off the lamp next to his side of the bed, sighing his relief when Jake did the same. This entire evening had been one of the oddest Levi had ever experienced in his thirty-one years on this planet, which was fucking saying something considering he'd grown up with Ruby.

He sighed, wishing he hadn't thought the f-word, then recalled the whole cock-whore comment and decided that wasn't very nice language, either.

This whole no-cussing thing was really freakin' hard!

The most frustrating thing of all was the undeniable fact that Levi would have given anything in that moment to have Jake wrap him up in his arms as they each drifted off to sleep. Levi had missed that part of being a couple more than the sex—though he apparently needed to work on getting more of that as well, considering he was currently getting an erection for absolutely no reason.

He forced his eyes shut, wishing he wasn't going to bed irritated, not to mention frustrated, sexually and otherwise. Wishing that he would stop making fucking wishes as well, considering none of them ever seemed to come true.

He sighed, exhaling dramatically. *God damn it, I just cussed again.*

CHAPTER EIGHT

The Rainbow Palace sat atop Wilde City Tower, on the eightieth floor. The ceilings stretched nearly twenty feet high, taking up what were technically the top two floors of the Art Deco skyscraper. The restaurant doubled as a nightclub, featuring a stage and dance floor in the center of the room with dining tables radiating out on all sides like smaller planets orbiting the sun. A monstrous crystal chandelier hung in the center of room, glittering in the natural light that poured in through the windows.

Levi stood staring out the massive ten foot high windows which offered breathtaking panoramic views of the cityscape. Its popularity had waned several times over the years, but the Palace always managed to come back stronger than ever, setting trends and forever harkening back to eras long gone but not forgotten.

Jake's loud barreling laugh ripped him out of his own thoughts.

Levi glanced down at his tablet, reviewing his notes thus far, while doing his best to remain focused on the task at hand. It was difficult to concentrate listening to Jake and Julia's incessant schoolgirl giggling. It was obvious they were each a bit tipsy as they sat patiently in the large dining room waiting for Armand Beauchene, baker and wedding-cake-maker extraordinaire, to finish setting up his exquisitely decorated samples.

"That man is a freakin' genius with icing," David Kramer, said, sidling up next to Levi who finished typing in the last of his notes thus far on his tablet. "Gorgeous, little cake-lettes of perfection."

David had been Levi's inside connection to the Rainbow Palace. He'd been the GM of the restaurant and adjoining Stratosphere bar on the opposite side of the building for the last ten years or so. David's long-time partner, Todd Everton, had been Dan's investment banker for years and had helped secure the funding for the boardwalk revitalization.

"It seems almost a shame to eat them, doesn't it?" Levi asked, staring at the elegant mini-cakes.

"I'll continue reminding myself of that." David frowned. "My waistline appreciates any and all abstinence from sugary baked goods."

Considering the man was rail-thin with zero percent body fat, it seemed an unlikely issue David had ever been faced with, which meant he was likely fishing for compliments.

"Are you kidding me, you look incredible, David." Levi looked him up and down. "You're either spending way too much time in the gym or you and Todd are working things off some *other* way?"

David's mouth fell open in faux-shock and awe. "You're too much, Levi Goode—*God* how I miss you. You were the first boyfriend of Dan's that I didn't want to stab in the face."

Levi coughed, choking on the swig of water he'd just taken.

"I'm sorry, that was mildly melodramatic."

"Only mildly?" Levi asked.

"You know what I mean, I can have an actual conversation with you and I haven't been able to say the same for many of Dan's other boy toys. I don't know where he finds them. Is there a 'Dumb and Full o' Cum Mart' that I've never heard of where you can find brainless Stepford studs?"

"I love you for saying that," Levi said, feeling a bit of a lift, having been referred to as a boy toy with brains, even though he knew deep down he shouldn't consider that a compliment. Still, once you turned thirty, the conditions on which compliments are judged become shorter.

"It's entirely selfish on my part, one more dinner party discussing creatine shakes and testosterone supplements and I'll kill myself." David sighed nudging his head toward Jake and Julia. "What's going on with you and the elusive Mr. Freeman?"

Levi stood up straight, wondering what the hell David meant by that. "Nothing."

"Well, *nothing* has looked over at least a dozen times since I walked up and started talking to you, my friend. Where I come from, that ain't nothing."

"We're friends, sort of… I think," Levi said, cringing as he wasn't actually one-hundred percent sure what they were.

"Did he split with that stick-up-his-butt boyfriend, Victor something or other?"

"There's nothing going on, David, Scout's honor." Levi held up two fingers. "And is there anyone who actually likes Victor?"

"That's the peace sign, dummy."

Levi scowled, trying in vain to recall what the actual Scout's honor gesture was.

"And have you met Victor?"

"Briefly," Levi said.

"Need I say more?" David asked.

Levi tried not to smile, wishing the fact no one liked Jake's boyfriend didn't fill him with quite so much glee.

David shook his head. "Just be careful."

"I would, if anything were going on, but since there isn't, I have nothing to worry about."

"You might wanna tell that to Mr. Dreamy-eyes over there, then."

He turned, walking away before Levi could make any other declarations of innocence and decided it was best to avoid looking at Mr. Dreamy-eyes at all costs.

A quick glance over at Armand and Levi could see they were almost ready to begin.

It had taken a little finagling on Levi's part to get Armand to do the tasting here. Normally people went to Armand, not the other way around, but the Freeman name carried a lot of weight, and like David, Armand had loathed Libby Washington, refusing to work with the woman, regardless of her amazing clientele list. Unfortunately for Libby, Armand's reputation went far beyond her long arm of retribution, as did the Rainbow Palace's.

Both had been able to diss Libby and come out on the other side unscathed.

Though he didn't need the business, per say, Armand was certainly aware that landing the Freemans as clients would be a feather in his cap, especially now that he'd no longer have to deal with Libby in order to work with the family. In turn, Levi was hoping this event would be the first of many he would organize featuring Armand's award winning pastries. He'd been especially forthcoming with the praise and compliments over Armand's brilliance since he'd arrived… nearly an hour late.

At this stage, they'd lost Gregory and his brother, Richard, to the Stratosphere bar on the opposite side of the building. Richard had flown in for the weekend from the Kingsley's European headquarters in London and while he seemed a jovial sort, he didn't appear to care much about helping his brother and sister-in-law settle the menu for their anniversary party. He also didn't share Gregory's leading-man, good looks, and while he could certainly see the family resemblance, Richard was a little more generic looking in comparison.

To their credit, the brothers had made it through the menu tasting, but the wine and champagne pairings had marked the end of their attention span—having left the cake selection up to Julia and Jake. Harold and Gloria were unable to attend the tasting as they had a prior commitment in D.C. Once he'd heard that, it made sense why Julia had been so insistent upon scheduling the tasting for this weekend. Apparently she was still holding a grudge over the whole Glennellen incident.

"Looks like we're almost ready to begin," Levi said as he passed by Jake and Julia on his way over to the buffet table where Armand had painstakingly arranged his array of beautifully decorated petite confections.

They each nodded back acknowledging Levi, while sipping on the last of the champagne. Julia punched Jake playfully in the arm. "Listen here, pally, I took a bullet for you by greedily hogging all the selfish genes when we were in the womb together, leaving little Jakey with only saintly goodness and light."

Jake scoffed at that and Julia began poking him in the sides making him giggle while he attempted to swat away her hands.

Levi was doing his best not to laugh at the two of them as he stepped up to shake hands with Armand.

"I'm not very saintly in the bedroom," Jake said, in a devilish tone, eyebrows wiggling.

Startled hearing that sort of declaration, Levi tripped over his own feet, falling into the table where all the cake samples had been laid out. His hand landed right on top of one of the perfectly iced confections and for a moment it was like time itself had stopped.

Armand let out a yelp, like he'd been physically wounded by seeing one of his precious creations squished under the weight of Levi's hand. David was standing at the other end of the table with his hand covering his mouth as he transitioned from gasp of horror to laughing under his breath.

Levi was completely mortified and slowly glanced up to see Armand glaring at him.

"I am *soooo* sorry, Armand." He carefully lifted his hand, the cake and icing mushed between his fingers, jumping slightly when the plate made a loud clang as it broke away and fell back onto the table.

Armand was pointing, his mouth agape while several versions of squeak came out.

"I've totally ruined it, I know. It's was an accident, I swear."

Julia was trying not to laugh, and failing miserably while Jake looked on, visibly amused.

"*Fils de pute*," Armand muttered, peering down at the card to see which one of his babies Levi had just murdered. "The amaretto almond crème with white chocolate ganache filling… this is my *signature* cake!"

Levi stood there, unable to move, his mouth hanging open, unsure what to say. "I'm—"

"But whatever, no big deal…" Armand said, his accent getting thicker the angrier he became. "What are you, Jerry Lewis? Catastrophe!"

"I am truly sorry. I tripped, Armand, please, *please* forgive me?"

"*Trou du cul,*" Armand muttered, still scowling at Levi.

He didn't understand French, but Armand's tone was dripping with sarcasm so he assumed it wasn't 'I forgive you'. Julia and Jake were both giggling, and not even bothering to try and hide the fact at this point.

"How they will be able to make an educated decision now, I do not know," Armand said, tossing his hands in the air.

"Let's all just calm down." Jake looked distractingly sexy, sauntering over to Levi and grabbing him by the wrist. "I got this."

Levi was confused for a moment thinking Jake was going to use the napkin in his other hand to help wipe the cake off. Instead, Jake lifted Levi's cake-caked hand up to his mouth and seductively took his index finger all the way into his mouth, slowly sucking it clean.

Levi was fairly certain he'd stopped breathing altogether and could see David was now looking at him smugly, most definitely not buying the whole 'we're just friends' bit. Jake stood there for a moment, chewing and moaning as if pondering the flavor before swallowing the mashed up baked-good.

Levi was doing his level best to not sprout wood as that had been the single most erotic thing anyone had ever done to him. That thought immediately made him sad. However, Jake's icing smeared mouth helped lighten the mood. He looked completely silly, smiling and nodding his head.

"That *is* good," Jake finally said, jerking Levi's hand out toward Julia. "You have to try this."

Armand was completely stunned and not the least bit pleased as Julia stood there, frozen in place. She was snickering but Levi could tell that in spite of however amusing she found all of this, her inner germ-a-phobe couldn't quite make the leap, allowing her to join in the finger-licking-fun.

"I'll take your word for it." She nodded, clinging to her champagne flute the way a toddler did their blanky.

"Your loss," Jake said, repeating the action by taking Levi's middle finger all the way into his mouth and slowly sucking the second finger clean.

Levi jerked his hand free not wanting to provide Jake with an opportunity to lick the rest of his hand. He was laughing nervously since there had been definite wood-sproutage following the second act.

"That is tasty," Jake said earnestly. "I see why it's so popular."

Armand was still scowling, but he forced some semblance of a smile. "Thank you, Mr. Freeman."

Levi was more grateful than words could ever express that Julia hadn't repeated her brother's actions as he was fairly certain he would never be able to look Julia Freeman-Kingsley in the face again had she sucked cake from his finger.

Levi forced a smile and sheepishly glanced over at Armand who still stared back at him like Levi was the Anti-Christ. "Awesome... *yay*... crisis averted. I'll just go wash my hands and we'll move on, 'kay everyone?"

They all nodded, and Jake was smiling at him in a manner which would no doubt get the man thrown out of many a garden party in polite society. He sucked down the last of the champagne from his glass and as much as Levi wanted to smack the crap out of him, Jake had been trying to help—in his own completely inappropriate way, mind you, but his heart had been in the right place.

That's what Levi decided the truth was going to be at any rate.

Levi snagged a cloth napkin off the table and placed it under his cake-hand so he wouldn't leave a crumb trail in his wake on the way to the restroom.

* * * *

The dim lighting and rich, dark finishes of the Rainbow Palace men's room felt comforting to Levi, who splashed some water on his face in an attempt to rinse his own embarrassment away. After that performance, he was finding it difficult to muster up the strength to go back out there and face everyone.

"Fucking humiliated," he muttered, still hearing Jake Freeman seductively saying the words, *I'm not very saintly in the bedroom*, over and over on a loop in the back of his mind.

"Ridiculousness." Levi patted his face dry with the paper towel and glanced up at his reflection in the mirror. "That was the single most idiotic thing you have ever done in your entire life. What the hell is wrong with you?"

He jumped, startled by the door swishing open to find Jake standing there, staring at him for a moment before walking over to the urinal. "Pretty sure that cake tasted ten times better served right from your hand."

The sound of Jake's zipper was all Levi heard, finding it difficult to breathe. Jake was most definitely flirting, but again, it was presumably under the guise of attempting to make Levi feel better about being a buffoon, which made it impossible to confront the man over. The fact that he didn't exactly hate having Jake flirt with him was so totally beside the point.

"That's sweet, though as a rule, party planners aren't supposed to smear the catering all over themselves."

Jake shrugged, his eyes slightly glazed as he glanced back over his shoulder at Levi. "I still say you added a certain zesty flavor that wouldn't have been there otherwise."

"Well, I'm a busy man, so I'm not sure I have time to run after you all day, fondling your food as you break for meals."

Jake chuckled, his head tilting sideways as he zipped back up and flushed the urinal. He didn't need to say anything. Levi could see it there, in Jake's eyes as he walked over to the sink and began washing his hands. Whatever attraction there was between the two of them, it wasn't going away, and judging by the expression on Jake's face as he hazily looked up at Levi, the man wanted to do deliciously depraved things to him.

"I suppose it might freak people out to see me licking food off your naked body in the hospital cafeteria or the nearest drive through lane."

How Levi had managed to become naked in this scenario was completely lost on him, and when he opened his mouth to speak, nothing came out. Instead, images of a naked Jake popped into Levi's version of this food-licking fantasy and it took all his concentration to purge the visual from his brain before his erection decided to return for an encore performance.

The discomfort must have been apparent because Jake took a step back after wiping his hands dry and tossed the paper towel in the trash.

"That was completely out of line for me to say," Jake said, visibly anxious and uncomfortable. "Wow, so sorry, Levi, please accept my apology. You must think me a total scumbag."

"No," Levi said, unable to move as if rooted to the damn floor. "You were just trying to make me feel better, right? At least, that's how I took it."

He heard Valarie's voice in the back of his head. *Liar, liar pants on fire.*

"Okay… cool… that's good, then," Jake smiled weakly. "Champagne went right to my head."

Which one?

Levi eyed Jake's crotch, momentarily contemplating the possibilities.

Stop! Stop that!! Sheesh!

Jake smiled, thumbing back toward the door. "I'm gonna go now."

"Thank God," Levi said, eyes widening when Jake paused, eyeing him suspiciously. "I meant *good* as in *okay…* I'll see ya out there, buddy."

Laughing, Jake shook his head. "We've got some work to do on the friendship front, I guess."

"It's looking that way," Levi said, his own tension relieved by Jake's candor. He then remembered the super-secret, special project he was setting up and sighed, wishing he didn't have to prolong this particularly awkward moment any longer. "Say, before you go, I wonder if I could ask a favor of you?"

"Sure, anything you need." Jake was standing awkwardly with a hand on the doorknob like he too might be desperate to escape.

"It's for Julia, for the party, but I want it to be a surprise and I'm afraid her PA might be uncomfortable with the intrigue."

"I'm listening," Jake said, his curiosity peaked.

"I need photographs, candid stuff of Julia and Gregory?"

"For what purpose?" Jake asked.

"I don't suppose you happened to catch the Darius Wertz exhibit over the summer?"

"The one down at the Prather Gallery?" Jake asked. "With the photographs projected up onto the giant silk sheeting?"

"That's the one," Levi said.

Jake nodded. "Yeah, so?"

"I know Wertz, sort of a friend of a friend thing, and he's agreed to help with the same sort of installation—it would be a private showing for Julia and Gregory, about Julia and Gregory—kind of a relationship retrospective."

"Why would you be doing this?" Jake asked, visibly confused.

Levi sighed, irritated that Jake didn't appear to trust him, which stung. "Something Julia said to me the first night we met, that to expect any semblance of romance during her anniversary was ludicrous—which is crazy, right? It's their anniversary, which is supposed to celebrate their love and commitment to one another."

Jake grinned, shaking his head in disbelief. "You are so great."

"Great, as in you'll help?" Levi asked, doing his best to look past the piercing, blue-eyed adorability Jake was firing his direction.

"I will, Levi. I'll touch base next week, and we can make a plan?"

Levi nodded, their gazes fixed onto one another before Jake finally turned and left the bathroom. Levi paused for a moment, taking in deep gulps of air while checking himself out in the mirror, pretending not to notice he had dirty in his eyes.

So much dirty he found it difficult to breathe.

"You are a bad, *bad* man, Levi Goode."

Dirty-eyed cake smasher.

CHAPTER NINE

As he surveyed the office, Levi was beginning to imagine a few more pieces falling into place. They'd hired three more employees over the past few weeks that had already started and he and Valerie had settled on three others who'd be coming in for their first day next week. The Thanksgiving holiday had thrown a bit of wrench into things since Goode City Event & Party Planning would only be open part of the week, but it would be enough time to get a feel for whether or not the newbies were going to work out.

He was unsure about one gal that started this past week, but the new receptionist, Caitlyn, was a firecracker. She'd come with loads of experience and had been instrumental in helping Levi and Valerie choose a phone and messaging system for the office that could also interface with their individual cell phones. They were still trying to work all the bugs out, but Caitlyn had single-handedly brought them out of the dark ages in under three days.

Then there was Angelo, who had also turned out to be a godsend. The man had not been lying when he'd said he was willing to do anything. He'd made coffee runs and helped Levi lug all the heavy party supplies left over from the cancer gala back into the storeroom—then took it upon himself to organize the storeroom—without being asked to. Beyond the benefit of being extra muscle, he also kept all the ladies in the office very happy. He was easy on the eyes, and on top of that, it was as if he put off some sort of pheromone that stunned everyone into a sort of hazy, state of bliss.

Most importantly, Angelo never said a word to Valerie about the whole Levi forcing him to be his pretend boyfriend debacle. She would have had a field day with that intel and he'd still be getting tortured by her for being such a dumbass. Levi typically berated himself enough for being an idiot as it was.

He powered down his computer and turned off his desk lamp, ready to call it a day. Between the ass he'd made of himself during the tasting at the Rainbow Palace earlier that day and the slew of meetings he'd had throughout the afternoon, he was ready for the weekend. Tomorrow he'd go check in on Ruby, but he had tonight to himself.

Nearly six o'clock on a Friday night and the only hot date he had lined up was with his right hand. On the bright side, at least his date planned to feed him some spicy Szechwan before trying to get into his pants.

"It's nice to be respected," he muttered, pulling on his coat as he headed toward the front door.

"Is that so?" Angelo asked, coming out of nowhere, scaring the shit out of Levi.

Thankfully he'd managed not to scream like a horror-movie-chick, but Levi's hand was now clasping his chest like he feared his heart might otherwise burst out of it.

"Christ, I thought you left already?"

Angelo thumbed back toward the bathroom. "I was changing." He held up a duffel as if offering further evidence that he was on the up and up. "Didn't mean to frighten you, though, sorry dude." He walked to his desk, stuffing the bag underneath.

"No, it's fine. Sorry, of course, you've got plans with friends, no doubt."

"I do, but not until later." Angelo weaved his way through the office, stopping next to Levi at the front door. "My apartment's all the way on the other side of town, though. Didn't want to go all the way home only to turn around and come back downtown later."

"Makes sense," Levi said, opening the door.

"I'm looking for a place closer, but it takes time to find when you're on a budget."

Angelo followed him out onto the sidewalk, waiting for Levi to lock the door.

"I'm headed off to find something to eat," Angelo said. "You could join me, assuming you don't already have plans."

"Um… sure, that sounds good," Levi said, motioning for Angelo to lead the way. "My treat?"

"You don't have to do that," Angelo said. "I invited you, remember."

"True, but I've done very little for my faux-boyfriend up until this point."

Angelo laughed as they headed south on Waterfront, which was fairly heavy with foot traffic by this time of night.

"Allow me to please apologize to you once again for that," Levi said, looking over at Angelo warily. "It was completely unprofessional for me to use you that way."

"I didn't mind," Angelo said, still grinning. "You have to know I think you're pretty hot by now. God knows I've flirted shamelessly."

"That's very kind of you to say, but completely unnecessary, Angelo. And dude, you flirt with everyone."

He laughed again. "Yeah, but I mean it with you."

"You're kind of a mess, aren't you?" Levi asked, pointing down the street. "Ever been to Batista's?"

"No, but I'm game for anything."

"It's nothing too adventurous, classic America cuisine, burgers, steaks and such?"

Angelo nodded. "Sounds good to me."

They each stopped at the next corner, waiting for the light to change.

"I'm just gonna throw this out there in the spirit of nothing ventured," Angelo said, not seeming to care who might overhear him. "I would be completely open to some good old fashioned fucking, you know, in the event you might be into that as well."

Levi watched the two ladies on the other side of Angelo smile at one another while pretending not to be eavesdropping.

"Who just up and says something like that?" Levi asked, feeling his face flush with heat.

"I'm not like an expert or anything, but in my vast experience thus far, the answer to your question would be, other gay men."

"I'm your boss, Angelo."

"And I'm propositioning you here, not the other way around," he said, following Levi who stepped off the curb to cross the street the second the light changed. "It's really not a big deal, Levi, I like to do what feels good—"

"And you think I'd feel good so you want to do me." Levi was laughing over the absurdity of the conversation. "I get it, I just can't believe it."

"It's just sex, Levi," Angelo said. "I'm not asking for your hand in marriage. I'm not asking for any kind of a commitment, actually."

"The old-fashioned-fucking bit pretty much made that clear."

"Oh, awesome," Angelo said.

"You know that if I agreed to the sex, I'd totally be using you?"

"I kinda picked up on that when you asked me to kiss you in an attempt to make 'The Jake' jealous."

"I'm *soooo* sorry, Angelo. God, I totally *suck*."

"That certainly sounds like a great way to make it up to me."

Levi smirked, slowing the pace down as they came upon the door to the restaurant.

"I have zero issues with you licking my wounds, I'm just sayin'."

"Will you please be serious?" Levi asked, opening the door.

Angelo walked into the restaurant, turning back to face Levi as he followed. "I never joke about blow jobs."

"Shhh, please stop saying... stuff like that! You're embarrassing me."

"I see that, it's kind of adorable," he said, lowering his voice.

"Oh my God, again with the flirting." Levi held up his hand to the hostess. "Table for two."

"You make flirting fun," Angelo whispered into his ear.

"You're incorrigible."

"Pulling out the big words, huh?" Angelo was looking him up and down with a lusty glare. "Please tell me incorrigible is like French for devastatingly handsome?"

Levi burst out laughing as the hostess told them it would be fifteen to twenty. They headed into the bar to wait.

"I'm begging you, Angelo, please behave yourself."

"Look, all I'm saying is I have no problem being the hot piece of meat you use to make your married boyfriend jealous."

Levi gasped. "I am not sleeping with Jake."

"Not yet, but I see the writing on the wall. I don't judge, Levi. Please feel free to use and abuse me in the meantime. I get off on that."

Levi was surveying the bar to see if there was any place for the two of them to sit. "I don't even know how to respond to that."

"That's cool, talking is overrated. Fucking on the other hand—"

Levi reached up and slapped a hand over Angelo's mouth, stifling anything else from spilling out from between those thick, pouty lips. The crowd parted as a large group of diners headed for the dining room because their table was ready. Levi froze, staring wide-eyed at Jake and Victor who were seated at a table right in front of them. They both stared up at Levi and Angelo. Jake was definitely surprised while Victor appeared to be amused.

Angelo mumbled something and Levi turned to see he was still standing there with his hand over Angelo's mouth.

Once the initial shock had worn off, Jake looked less than excited to see them. "Hello."

Levi slowly removed his hand from Angelo's mouth, faux laughing as he smacked Angelo playfully on the cheek before shoving his hand into his pants' pocket.

"Hello," Angelo said, grinning at Jake and Victor.

"Honey, you remember Jake, right?" Levi said, feeling the sweat collect under his arms.

"I do," Angelo said, taking a few steps over and shaking Jake's hand, then Victor's once Jake introduced them.

"Waiting for a table." Levi shrugged, unsure what to say once the introductions were out of the way.

"I assumed as much," Jake said, dryly.

"You should join us." Victor motioned toward the two empty chairs at their table.

"Thanks, that would be great," Angelo said, preventing Levi from declining the invite. He began removing his coat, stopping long enough to pull out a chair for Levi. "Take a load off, baby."

Levi was smiling while shooting hate-daggers from his eyes at Angelo. Reluctantly he began removing his coat, which Angelo jumped in to help him out of.

"He's so attentive," Levi said, faux-laughing again as he sat down.

"I like taking care of my man." Angelo winked at Jake and Victor.

Levi desperately grabbed for the cocktail waitress as she passed by the table and ordered a vodka tonic for himself. Angelo asked for Heineken, which is what Jake was drinking and Victor ordered them another round.

"Nice seeing you again, Victor," Levi said, praying that sounded somewhat earnest.

"You as well." Victor smiled, appearing mildly confused. "Apologies, but where did we meet again?"

"You met at Julia's a few weeks ago," Jake reminded him.

Why bother taking the time to remember the help?

Victor smacked his hand against the tabletop. "The party planner!"

"That's me," Levi said, scrunching up his face like he found Victor adorable.

"He'd just flown back into town that morning," Jake said, as if having read Levi's judgey little mind.

Victor took a sip from his wine glass. "I was a bit jet lagged."

"He's been traveling a lot lately." Jake glared at his boyfriend.

"He's mad because I won't be around for Thanksgiving this year," Victor whispered, trying to play it off like Jake was being the unreasonable party. "Business meeting in Japan, which I unfortunately can't reschedule."

Jake looked unamused and Levi got the sense they'd been quarreling. Levi also felt like Victor might be uncomfortable discussing the topic which is what drove the man to awkwardly blurt everything out there.

"Since someone won't take time away from work to join me for an impromptu holiday in Japan," Victor added, "we're left at an impasse."

Or not so uncomfortable.

"You'll be in meetings all day, Victor. If I'm going to spend the holiday by myself, I'd prefer to be in my own home instead of sitting in a hotel room in a foreign country where I don't even speak the language."

"So, how's the anniversary extravaganza planning going?" Victor asked, changing the subject.

"Great, everything's humming right along." Levi was startled slightly when Angelo placed his arm around his shoulder.

Jake's eyebrows hitched seeming to take notice of his reaction, and thankfully the cocktail waitress showed up with their drinks.

"You can put all this on our tab," Victor said.

"No, you don't have to—"

"It's our pleasure," Jake said, cutting Levi off.

"You two should join us for dinner," Victor announced, his tone coming off more like a demand.

Jake crossed his arms and sat back in his seat and Levi took that as a definite sign to decline.

"What do you think, baby?" Angelo leaned over and kissed Levi on the cheek before looking at Victor. "I was planning on getting him all liquored up so I could drag him back home and take advantage of him in his weakened state."

Victor laughed.

Jake smiled. "Well, far be it for us to interrupt your romantic evening out, right honey?"

"Sure, of course," Victor said. "We've certainly had our fair share of those over the years."

"I'm actually not feeling too good, babe." Jake pushed his untouched beer over to Angelo. "Let's pay the tab and head home."

"Okay." Victor sighed, grabbing his wine glass and taking it with him as he headed to the bar.

Angelo shrugged, accepting the extra beer. "Thanks."

"Please excuse us." Jake looked a little sad as he got up from the table. "Hope we didn't put a damper on your evening."

He was staring at Levi, who wasn't quite capable of looking away. He wanted to get up and give Jake a hug or something.

"No problem," Angelo finally said, after too long of a pause in the conversation passed by. "You should see the way this one lays into me when he's angry."

Jake glanced back and forth between the two of them as he slipped on his coat. "Right, sure."

Angelo ran his thick, long fingers through the back of Levi's hair. "Of course the making up is so much fun."

"Ready?" Victor asked, coming back to the table.

Jake nodded but said nothing else as they walked off and disappeared into the crowd hovering around the hostess station.

"That wasn't the least bit awkward."

Levi rolled his eyes as Angelo preened, visibly pleased with his performance. Of course, Levi was too preoccupied, worrying about Jake and feeling crummy over how sad the man appeared to be. Worse yet, he couldn't seem to keep himself from feeling bad for Victor, as well. It was painfully obvious he wanted to please Jake and while there had been a certain dryness to his personality, Levi didn't find him to be as uppity as David seemed to imply.

Underneath everything else were the feelings of guilt Levi was experiencing over how much he cared for Jake. He closed his eyes and made a silent plea for the universe to please make his feelings for Jake go away once and for all.

Pretty please?

* * * *

Levi grunted, yanking on the large metal barn-style door and flicked on the light as he entered his loft. He signaled for Angelo to please come inside, pulling the door closed behind them. The small, informal entry lead into the open kitchen, dining and living areas on one side and the hallway that led back to the bedrooms in the opposite direction.

"What time are you meeting your friends?" Levi asked, turning on the overhead lights in the kitchen.

"Around nine-thirty or ten," Angelo muttered, walking into the living room. "Were you robbed or something?"

Levi opened the fridge to see what he might have to drink. "No, I know, it's kinda sparse at the moment. Haven't really had much time to spend personalizing the space. I've got vodka with pretty much nothing to mix it with and beer, though I don't know how long that's been there." He cringed. "Does beer go bad?"

"How long have you lived here?" Angelo asked, removing his coat.

Levi sighed. "Too long to not have this place furnished already, I know. I've heard it plenty from Valerie."

"Beer does go bad, but it's usually okay for a year or two if it's stored correctly," Angelo said, tossing his coat onto one of the bar stools sitting along the large island. "I'm just surprised because you're pretty organized downstairs with the office stuff. This doesn't track with my impression of you."

"Beer it is!" Levi passed Angelo a bottle deciding to make the decision for him since he was too busy marveling over Levi's flawed personal life, which was admittedly, in shambles at the moment.

"Do you at least have a trash can?" he asked, twisting the cap off the bottle.

"Under the sink, smart ass," Levi said, grabbing a beer for himself, considering it apparently wasn't going to be viable for consumption for too many more months.

"Wow," Angelo said, taking in the view of the water from the row of large windows across the front of the building. "I was about to say this place seemed large for one person, with so little personal possessions, but with this view I'm thinking none of that matters."

Levi smiled, nodding as he rounded the island and stood next to Angelo who was staring out at the world beyond this room.

"I like it more during the day. Of course I'm rarely here to enjoy it."

Angelo turned to face him, taking a step closer as Levi grinned, taking a step back.

"I didn't ask you up for that," Levi said, stumbling backward until Angelo had him backed up against the kitchen island, blocking any chance of escape by placing an arm on the countertop on either side of Levi.

"You are so sexy," Angelo said, leaning in close enough for Levi to feel the man's breath across his face.

Levi decided to close his eyes and let the kiss he knew was forthcoming happen, regardless of any previous objections. As their lips met, he opened his mouth, accepting Angelo's tongue. The man was certainly an expert kisser, and Levi was taken aback by how slow and sensual Angelo was. Quite different from the down and dirty kiss they shared at Glennellen. Levi fell prey to the way Angelo made him feel, his entire body was on fire with the needy want of skin on skin—wet tongues licking, mouths sucking and the feel of another man's hard body pressing against his.

Levi got all that from just one kiss. The one thing he'd been hoping to find was unfortunately missing. He allowed the kiss to deepen, feeling Angelo undoing the buttons of his shirt, allowing his hands to slip inside the fabric, fingertips pressing into his skin.

Angelo groaned when Levi placed a hand on his chest, mistaking it for a sign that he should keep going.

"Wait," Levi said, trying to catch his breath and shake the lusty haze from his head.

"Let make you feel good, Levi," Angelo said, lightly kissing and gently sucking on his ear lobe and neck.

"I can't Angelo. Thank you for wanting to… but I can't," Levi said, his head telling him to push the man away while his body yearned for just the opposite.

The palm of Angelo's hand pressing against his erection, had his eye lids fluttering as his vision went slightly hazy. "I can help you forget about him for a little while."

That was exactly the problem, Levi thought, twisting out of the embrace and taking a few steps away for much needed distance from the heat. He heard Angelo curse under his breath.

"I shouldn't have mentioned Jake."

Levi laughed, seeing that he appeared to be genuinely upset with himself.

"I'm glad you find that humorous," Angelo added, adjusting the rather large bulge in his jeans.

"I'm not laughing at you, just so incredibly flattered that you want to have sex with me that badly."

"Flattered in the sense you feel bad enough to go ahead and take off all your clothes so we can fuck each other's brains out?" he asked, with a hopeful expression on his face.

Levi frowned, hating that he was about to burst the bubble of one of the most beautiful men he'd ever laid eyes.

"Wow, really?" Angelo asked, looking particularly dumbfounded. "This has never happened to me before."

He wasn't proud of the fact that he'd just used the man again, but in all fairness, in this particular instance, Levi had been praying that one kiss from Angelo would be enough to blast away any and all feelings he had for Jake. Granted, it wasn't the smartest plan, considering if that had happened

Levi would then probably just fall for Angelo, who had made it relatively clear that he was only looking for fun.

Either way, it would've been out of the frying pan and into the fire for Levi. That didn't mean he enjoyed seeing the man all turned on with no relief in sight.

"I could give you a hand job?" Levi offered, thinking that would be something at least.

Angelo paused, seeming to actually consider that for a moment, then sighed, a scowl taking over his face. "No, forget it, you're not into it."

Levi cringed, not really able to deny that. "But I feel bad for getting you all worked up."

He exhaled, grabbing his beer off the countertop and taking a long swig. "I should go."

"You don't have to," Levi said, feeling like a shit-heel.

"I really do." Angelo took another big swig. "If I stay, I'll try and use that guilt of yours to get you into bed. As much as I'd love to have sex with you, I don't want to be something you regret later. That would likely make working together uncomfortable."

"All right, I get that." Levi didn't really want him to go, but since he couldn't offer the man the one thing he wanted, it didn't seem fair to keep him there. "Thank you again, for understanding, for joining me for dinner, for being my fake boyfriend—all of it. You're a damn fine friend, Angelo."

"I really hate that about me," he said, a cheeky half smile forming.

"I've never been very good at the 'just sex' thing anyway," Levi said as Angelo headed for his coat.

"I seriously doubt that," Angelo said, frowning. "No one who kisses the way you do is going to be bad in bed."

With that he leaned in and planted one last soft peck on the lips, before groaning painfully and heading toward the door.

They said goodnight and Levi pulled the door closed, not kidding himself for one minute that Angelo wouldn't walk into the first bar and find himself drowning in a multitude of other offers from guys who would happily worship at the Angelo altar.

He went back to the kitchen and poured out what was left of the beers, rinsing it down the sink before tossing the bottles in the recycling bin. He turned off all the lights and headed straight to bed—wishing he could stop thinking about Jake Freeman.

CHAPTER TEN

Levi slowed to a stop in front of Ruby's bungalow, wondering who the car in her driveway belonged to. His mother maintained a steady rotation of gentleman friends whom she 'dated' whenever she felt well enough to entertain company. Ruby loved getting dolled up and going out to dinner or even dancing on the occasions she was up to it. She was never so alive as when she was dancing. The instant she began moving across the dance floor, it was as if someone switched on some sort of inner light that turned her into a beacon. Inevitably, any onlookers found themselves completely entranced by her.

Levi was also susceptible to the phenomena. No matter how angry or ashamed he ever found himself over her behavior, the fact that entire world would stop to watch his mother when she danced was a source of pride for him. It was the thing that made her special and justified much of her arrogant, often stubborn behavior.

The flip side of no longer being able to do the one thing that set Ruby apart from all other mere mortals were the bouts of depression that periodically took her over. Seeing his mother retreat within herself frightened Levi. It was as if something snuffed out that inner light for a while. She wasn't suicidal, but watching Ruby stumbling through the day, just going through the motions broke Levi up inside.

Getting out of his car, he realized how long it had been since he'd taken Ruby out on the town and decided that needed to be corrected soon—assuming she could squeeze him in somewhere.

The next best thing to dancing for Ruby, was receiving the undivided attention of an attractive man. It was that type of focused attention that Levi had never been personally comfortable with, which is partially why being around Jake made him feel slightly off-kilter. Ruby fed off that kind of attention and he'd always envied her that. Levi feared having a guy look too closely would only reveal all the flaws that were hiding under the surface—as if all the unbecoming parts of who he was would rise to the surface and present themselves like tattoos across his skin. It made him feel vulnerable, like he had no control and frankly, he'd suffered enough wayward, fly-by-the-seat-of-your-pants kind of behavior during his childhood.

Walking through the front door and entering Ruby's house, Levi could hear the hysterical laughter. He froze, hearing Jake's voice, along with another he didn't recognize. Before he'd been able to react in time to stop it, the heavy wooden front door closed behind him, making a loud thud.

Dam—arn it.

The laughter stopped as Ruby called out, "Hello, who has dared entered my domain?"

Levi rolled his eyes, fully aware his mother had her inner-diva on, judging by the tone in her voice.

"It's me, Momma!" Levi poked his head around the corner so he could be seen.

"Hey!" Jake sounded too happy to see him. "Wasn't expecting to see you."

He wanted to flee, but didn't dare, fearing Ruby would instantly know that he was in love with Jake.

"Odd considering Ruby knew I was coming over this morning." Walking through the kitchen, Levi spotted the owner of the third voice. He said his hellos to everyone, taking the two steps down into the living room.

"Like I can keep track of your crazy schedule," Ruby said, looking at her new friend. "My son is a very busy boy."

Jake stood up off the sofa and crossed the room, giving Levi a bear hug that he didn't initially want yet admittedly also didn't want to be released from. Having Jake's arms around him was incredible—the warmth from his hard body radiated into Levi. It was heaven on Earth. Jake seemed to be aware of that fact considering he allowed Levi to hang on longer than what would typically be considered appropriate for friends.

Levi knew he needed to release Jake, but his body didn't seem to agree with his brain. He closed his eyes for a fraction of a second, breathing in Jake's spicy aftershave mixed with the naturally awesome scent of the man himself, attempting to commit it to memory before finally letting go.

He was immediately embarrassed as Ruby and the stranger exchanged a knowing glance, something Jake took note of as well, considering the awkward shuffling of arms that ended in his usual, cross-armed defensive stance.

"So what's going on here?" Levi asked, attempting to draw the attention away from himself.

"Right, sorry," Jake stammered, motioning toward the judgey interloper. "This is my good friend, Keith."

Levi shook Keith's hand, well sort of, considering Keith offered it to him in a 'kiss the ring of the benevolent' sort of way. Jake chuckled as he watched the exchange and Ruby looked at Levi like he'd lost his mind.

"Keith is a nurse—" Jake paused, watching as Keith's head cocked to the side with a 'no he didn't' expression on his face. "—an incredibly, fantastic, totally kick-ass, nurse... who is currently looking for a new client. As soon as I got wind of that information I immediately thought of Ruby."

"Oh!" Levi was intensely interested after hearing that. He took a seat in the pink, velvet upholstered parlor chair across from the sofa where Jake and Ruby were perched and smiled sweetly at Keith, hoping his desperation wasn't showing.

"Keith is also one of the legendary *Masquerade de Cabaret* Club female impersonators, DaVeena DaMore." Ruby was using one of her overtly exaggerated femme fatale impersonations. "Absolutely fabulous, darling."

Levi chuckled over the performance Ruby was putting on and stared up at the ceiling thinking the name sounded familiar. "You took me there for my eighteenth birthday?"

"I did, indeed." Ruby winked at Keith and Levi glanced over at Jake, wondering if that fact made him a little sad, considering the relationship he had with his own mother. "Ms. DaMore was one of the entertainers we saw that evening."

Levi's eyes widened. "Not Diana Ross?"

"Exactly," Ruby said, pointing at Levi.

Keith was visibly pleased that Levi remembered him.

"You were amazing," Levi said, "everyone one was good mind you, but when you stepped out onto that stage—"

"We both thought you *were* Diana Ross!" Ruby said cutting him off. "We nearly came out of our seats!"

Levi nodded as if Ms. DaMore might require him to confirm Ruby's version of events.

"I was very good… in my day. I did a mean Donna Summer as well, but my Lady Ross was money. No one could touch me."

"That was a good night," Levi said, touched by a bout of nostalgia.

Ruby smiled at him. "The night you told me you were gay."

"Which you'd already figured out, considering where you'd taken me to celebrate my birthday."

"I wanted you to know it was okay—that I'd love you no matter what."

"You were damn lucky to have a mom who was so accepting," Jake said.

He and Ruby stared at one another for several seconds as Levi remembered how relieved he'd been once he'd finally come out to her. To the outside world, it might have seemed like a foregone conclusion that Ruby would be the type of free-spirited mother who'd be accepting of his homo-ness. From his teen-angst-perspective at that time, his mother had been anything but predictable and for that reason, he'd been nervous.

"Which is certainly something that makes working with Miss Ruby attractive for me," Keith said.

Levi nodded, understanding how not having to hide who he was from an employer would be appealing. No one was going to appreciate ALL of who Keith was more than Ruby. Keith could show up each day dressed as DeVeena and Ruby would be ecstatic. On the surface it seemed like a match made in heaven and Levi could see that Ruby was actually excited by the prospect. It was the first time she'd ever looked at anyone with an RN after their name and didn't think—*enemy.*

"Though I don't entertain much these days," Keith added, addressing Levi once again. "They bring me back for special events and I do several charity functions throughout the year, but I've otherwise been unceremoniously placed out to pasture, so to speak."

"Something else we have in common," Ruby said, begrudgingly.

Jake cleared his throat. "If I may, I feel like I should point out that Keith is in high demand, Levi. He came here to meet Ruby as a favor to me, but you should know that there's a lengthy list of people who are clamoring for his services."

Levi nodded, letting Jake know he understood the score and sat quietly, listening as Keith ran through his list of terms, including a pay rate that was considerably more than what Levi had been paying through the home-health service. Though having someone he could count on to be there for Ruby, that peace of mind would be worth the extra dough. Keith's list of references were numerous and all glowing— having Jake vouch for him also carried a lot of weight. Keith was also completely candid about the fact much of his clientele in the past had been hospice or palliative care and that working with Ruby would be a welcome break from that.

"Please don't misunderstand me." Keith raised a hand and sat up a little straighter in his chair. "It is extremely rewarding, helping patients cross over between life and death with some semblance of dignity—as is knowing I've made a difference in the lives of the family members who are left behind, but it is equally a very emotional experience."

Levi nodded, able to empathize to a degree. Though the occasions were certainly incomparable, Levi's clients also allowed him into their lives during some of the most personal and private milestones. Levi derived a certain amount of pride from making those moments special and memorable.

"Working with Miss Ruby would be a ... that for me," Keith continued. "That being said, ...ite from completely honest with each of you." Keith glanced b... will be Ruby and Levi. "I am a very opinionated individual a... call a spade a spade. I do not temper those opinions t... anyone. If you don't like what I have to say, that is fine, just don't expect me to apologize. End of the day, I will always act in the best interest of my patient."

Levi glared at Ruby, as if to say, *you gonna be okay with that?*

She was visibly displeased by the unspoken accusation.

"I'm sorry, but my mother can be… stubborn and likely, equally opinionated—"

"I tell the truth as I see it," Keith said, cutting Levi off, "but I have no patience for hypocrisy, so the bright side is I won't begrudge you or Miss Ruby the same."

"Which seems completely fair to me," Ruby clarified, for the record.

Levi sighed, nodding. "If this is what you want, Momma—"

"It is," Ruby said, firmly.

"—then it's what I want, too."

Keith grinned, eyes glinting as he winked at Ruby who looked like a giddy school girl that just got asked to the prom. Levi relaxed a bit more, noting that Keith seemed equally excited by the prospect of working with his mother. He found himself getting slightly emotional, all that added tension he'd been carrying around for weeks beginning to ease.

With any luck, this would be the last time he'd ever need to hire a nurse for Ruby. As that realization sank in, Levi turned toward Jake, who was laughing as Ruby and Keith exchanged carpy barbs back and forth. This was the man responsible for making his mother happier than Levi had seen her a very long time.

"Levi, perhaps you could go make some coffee for one?" Ruby asked. "My apologies, to you all, had I been aware of all the lovely company I'd have this morning I would've been better prepared."

"I'm afraid that's my fault," Jake said, apologetically. "I ran into Keith unexpectedly and things unfolded quickly."

"It was so kind of you to think of me, Jake," Ruby said, staring at Jake with so much admiration that it physically wounded Levi. He winced as he stood to go make the coffee. "Such a sweet boy this one is, Levi. Jake has come by to check on me several times, you know?"

Levi didn't know that considering neither Jake nor Ruby had mentioned it before now.

"I'll be right back." Levi forced a smile as he headed for the safety and solitude of the kitchen.

He kept his back to the three of them as he went about making the coffee, trying but failing to maintain his composure. He tried to concentrate on the set of pink, tutu-wearing, dancing piglet figurines that had reigned supreme—happily displayed on the white painted kitchen window sill since the day Ruby had unpacked them after relocating here from Vegas. They'd always made him feel better when he'd been sad or afraid as a child, but the silly, whimsical quality didn't seem to be much help at the moment.

Levi felt a lone, traitorous tear running down his cheek and he cursed the little bastard for daring to defy his wishes. It was all Jake's doing, damn it. All those years he'd spent carefully constructing the imaginary moat meant to protect his heart, had been all for naught. Jake had managed to

traverse it with little to no effort at all–
walk on water, yet would never truly be Len who could

No one had ever looked after him and For.
up, not truly. There'd been a few men that Ruby owing
back in the day who had made surface attempts at beed
man' in their lives, but for the most part it had been the
of them against the world. But now, here was this man-
whom he loved with his whole heart but couldn't be with.
This man who expected nothing in return for these random
acts of kindness because there was nothing Levi could offer
him, aside from the friendship he'd already reluctantly given.

That tore him up inside because deep down, Levi knew
why Jake was doing it.

"Can I help?" Jake asked quietly from behind him.

Levi sniffed, attempting to stealthily wipe his cheek with
his shoulder, not wanting Jake to see he was crying. "Sure,
you can grab some cups from the cabinet if you don't mind."

Levi pointed at the appropriate cabinet without turning
to look Jake in the eye, fearing that would be the end of him.

"Hope I didn't overstep by bringing Keith over without
checking with you first. It was all very spur of the moment.
The instant I saw Keith I thought of Ruby and before I
knew it, we were on her doorstep."

Levi nodded, still not able to face him. "It's fine, Jake.
I'm grateful to you for continuing to keep an eye on her. I
didn't know you were doing that, but it means the world to
me that you have."

He could hear Jake attempting to quietly remove the
cups from the cabinet, well aware the man was staring a hole
into the side of Levi's head. Levi watched the coffee maker,
listening to it gurgle as the water began heating up.

". me, then?" Jake asked. "Please, Levi, won't you not upset with me."

I need to see sucking in a deep gulp of air as he turned, Levi either betrayal as tear number two went rolling feeling her cheek. He could see the fear on Jake's face, down Levi was upset with him.

"Damn it, I suck," Jake whispered, peering into the other room, visibly aware they would be able to overhear them if he spoke too loudly.

Levi shook his head. "You're totally anti-sucky."

He pointed toward the dining room, brushing past Jake, wanting to make sure Ruby couldn't see him. He wiped his face and steadied himself, irritated that Jake had seen him like this, but he didn't want Ruby to know how stressed he'd been, worrying about what they were going to do in the event he couldn't secure another full-time nurse to help care for her.

"I know you've been worried about Ruby, I just wanted to help—"

"Thank you, Jake." Levi cut him off, feeling his eyes welling up again, but managing to keep the actual tears at bay. "This was above and beyond anything I could have ever asked from… anyone."

"Hey, Levi, please don't. We're friends, right?"

He nodded, smiling over the 'F' word, which had begun to feel more like their own secret replacement for the 'L' word, which neither of them could use due to the fact their feelings for one another were completely inappropriate. That familiar mix of shame, regret and undeniable affection danced across the man's face as those emotions played out there. Levi recognized them immediately having seen them there so often on his own face each time he looked in the mirror.

"I've been terrified of having the conversation with her about selling this house, which we'd very likely need to do in order to purchase one of the empty floors in my building to move her into."

Jake shook his head. "I take it she wasn't going to love that idea?"

"Hate would be more appropriate." Levi resisted the urge to reach out and take Jake into his arms. "I love you..."

Jake took in a deep breath when Levi trailed off, as if Levi had knocked the wind out of him.

"...for doing this, I mean," Levi clarified, despite the fact it had felt incredible to speak those three words aloud. "...and for continuing to check in on her."

"Don't be mad at her about that, I kinda asked her not to mention it to you."

"Why?" Levi asked, only confused for a moment. "Oh, right."

"You know I like Miss Ruby, quite genuinely," Jake said. "I didn't want you to think I was coming by for any other reason."

Levi nodded, hating how much loving Jake hurt. "Well, we should get back to the coffee, I guess."

Jake grabbed his arm as he tried to walk away and they stood like that for a moment, staring into one another's eyes.

Levi found it difficult to catch his breath.

Jake reached up, gently brushing his fingers across Levi's cheek before taking Levi behind the neck and pulling him into a tight embrace. Levi stood there, arms dangling lifelessly at his sides for a moment before the desire to hug Jake back became more than he could stand. As his hands slowly slid around Jack's waist, the ache in his chest grew, radiating outward like a throbbing pulse that threatened to end all of Levi.

In that brief moment, the ecstasy of holding Jake mixed with the agony that he would never have anything more, and in that split second, Levi's resolve weakened to the extent he would have done the unspeakable had they not been two rooms away from his mother.

Levi could feel Jake's heart beating through his chest, wondering if the thumpa-thumpa rhythm was occurring more rapidly than it typically did. His own heartbeat had quickened and the heat radiating into his body was addictive. Levi found himself yearning to experience this for always. Jake inhaled deeply, his face planted firmly in the crook of Levi's neck, like he might be trying to breathe Levi inside, keeping a tiny piece of him locked away there.

That idea seemed very romantic to him in that moment and Levi was once again acutely aware that he was not alone in his desperation to hold onto any part of the man in his arms—Jake felt the same for him. The heat of his breath and the stubble from his chin, Levi wanted to experience that over every inch of his skin—to imagine what that might feel like was so exquisite, and he held onto that sensation, thinking he might be able to live off of it for months, possibly even years if he was lucky.

As they finally parted, Levi plastered on the same grin that had become the mask he wore so often, as of late. They headed back into the kitchen to finish the chore Ruby had requested of Levi, not speaking a word to one another again.

Time to go back to the real world, Levi thought, as he followed Jake back into the living room with the tray of coffee and accoutrements—his sadness retreating back down to that place where Levi managed to shove all of life's disappointments.

CHAPTER ELEVEN

Freezing as he hovered outside Julia and Gregory's building, Levi adjusted the strap of his leather messenger bag with one hand, clutching a drink holder filled with Starbucks in the other. Checking his watch and beginning to worry as Jake was now nearly ten minutes late, he admitted to himself that this was not the way he wanted to kick off Thanksgiving Day.

It was a little after seven a.m. and all he wanted to do was crawl back into bed.

Miserable day, he thought, glancing upward at the overcast sky.

Julia and Gregory were in San Francisco for the holiday visiting Gregory's parents, and according to Jake, all their staff would also be off until Monday. Levi started dancing in place in an attempt to raise his body temperature, wishing that this hadn't been the only day Jake had been able to help him with the whole Darius Wertz anniversary surprise Levi had planned. Unfortunately, Jake was supposed to work over most of the weekend and from the sound of it, he'd be plenty busy between the holiday and all the Black Friday nonsense. Levi understood hard work and long hours but Jake's schedule sounded particularly brutal, working twenty-four hour shifts with a day or two off in between.

Either way, it was today or never and as far as Levi was concerned, never wasn't an option. Aside from not having the opportunity to sleep in, this early morning adventure wasn't going to interfere with the Goode family holiday tradition of Chinese take-out and old movies. He wasn't due at his mother's until one that afternoon, but he was supposed to pick up the food on his way out to Ruby's, so they were on a bit of deadline.

A taxi came screeching to a halt in front of the Wilkes Regency building and Levi watched wide-eyed as Jake tossed money over the seat and flew out of the back seat.

"I am so sorry, Levi," Jake said, stress pouring off of him in waves. "I completely overslept."

Levi smiled, hoping to put the man at ease. "It's fine, Ja—"

"It's not fine, you've no doubt been standing out here freezing to death for fifteen minutes or more."

It had been closer to twenty because he'd been early, as usual. "I was totally late, myself."

Jake stopped, staring intently into Levi's eyes, so much so that Levi felt himself taking a step back.

"You're lying," Jake declared. "To save me from feeling bad, no doubt, but totally lying."

Without giving Levi time to utter any sort of response, Jake grabbed him by the hand and took off for the entrance of the building, dragging Levi behind him.

"You have got to settle down," Levi whispered as they breezed past the doorman who waved at Jake, wishing them a pleasant holiday. "Preferably before ripping my arm out of socket."

Jake stopped at the elevator bay and anxiously punched the button. Now that they'd been forced to stop moving for more than two seconds, Levi could sense something was wrong—something aside from Jake's tardiness.

"Are you okay?" Levi asked.

He sighed, shaking his head that he wasn't, then said, "I don't wanna talk about it."

Levi could feel his forehead scrunching up, not happy with that but decided to let it slide for now. He held up the cup caddy with four Starbucks cups. "Coffee?"

Jake eyed the cups, then sniffed, breathing in the scent before finally nodding. "That would be great, thank you, Levi."

"I didn't know how you took your coffee, but—"

"I take it any way I can get it," Jake clarified, finally smiling a little, noting the way Levi had taken his comment. "That would be a coffee-specific trait."

Levi laughed, more pleased than he should've been over making Jake forget about whatever was troubling him, however briefly the joy lasted. The elevator doors opened and they each got in. Levi passed him a cup, waiting for Jake to punch the button that would take them all the way to the top floor. Jake moaned softly, taking that first sip as he leaned back against the wood-paneled wall. Levi made a mental note of that sound, having intensely enjoyed hearing it.

By the time they'd made their way inside the apartment and situated themselves in Julia's home office—where she kept all her meticulously organized photo albums that were arranged on bookshelves by year—Jake had begun to relax. Levi could still sense something was up with him, but he decided not to pry, assuming it might have something to do with Victor. That conjured up the recollection of Jake being alone for the holiday.

Jake was watching Levi feed some of Julia and Gregory's wedding photos through the scanning wand. "That's a handy little device."

"Darius gave it to me to use. It has an internal drive that stores all the scans so there's no computer needed."

"Speaking of." Jake walked around the desk and sat down at Julia's computer. "She's got a copy of their wedding video on here. I can copy that into a zip file if you have a thumb drive on you."

"That'd be great." Levi grabbed his bag off the floor and fished out a drive. "What are your plans for later?"

Jake stiffened, not looking up from the computer screen. "I was invited to Craig and Sophia's—my partner on the wagon and his wife."

"What the hell's a wagon?" Levi asked.

He smiled. "What we call the ambulance."

"Oh… groovy." Levi smirked, feeling like he'd just been allowed behind the secret EMT curtain.

Jake chuckled, shaking his head which made Levi think the man knew what he'd been thinking and was now making fun of him.

"So you're going to Craig and Sophia's then?" Levi asked.

Jake shrugged. "Not in the mood to be around a ton of people and they have a huge extended family."

Levi opened his mouth and Jake cut him off at the pass. "I appreciate the offer you're about to make, but I think I'd be better off hanging by myself this year—not in much of a celebratory mood today."

"Won't you please tell me what's wrong?" Levi fed another picture through the scanner. "It's only fair, damn it you stick your big, helpful nose in all my personal biddness."

Jake continued tapping keys on the computer and using the mouse but said nothing.

Levi sighed, signaling his disappointment. "Of course, perhaps we're not as good of friends as you've been making us out to be?"

Jake stopped typing and rolled his eyes. "Wow, that's a low blow."

"Sorry, Double-standard-Debbie, but friendship is a two way street."

Jake smiled, staring at Levi for a moment. "It's work-related stuff."

Levi motioned around the room, which they'd already made a mess of. "As opposed to *my* work-related stuff for which I've happily enlisted your help?"

"I don't want to drag you into my personal crap."

"You're not, Jake. For Christ's sake, I'm attempting to dive right into the muck, in case you hadn't noticed. So come out with it now or listen to me whine incessantly until you cave in and tell me anyway."

The expression on his face went dark again, the way he'd looked in the elevator earlier. "You catch any of the reports on the news yesterday about the thirty-three car pile-up on the interstate?"

Levi nodded when Jake glanced up at him.

"We were called out on that," he said, his voice getting softer.

Levi instantly felt like crap for pushing him, recalling there had been a high number of casualties.

"There was a kid... a boy... only nine years old," Jake said, rubbing his eyes.

Levi now knew why he'd slept through his alarm. He'd very likely not slept much, if at all.

"The kids, man, they're the toughest, you know?" Jake asked.

"I can imagine."

"The mom had been thrown from car. She was in bad shape but he was trapped inside the car. I sat with him, lying on top of the car which had been turned up on its side, sandwiched in between two other vehicles. It was just me and the kid, waiting for the fire department to get to us—needed to cut him out of the car."

"They couldn't just rip the door off and shimmy down in there and pull him out?" Levi asked.

Jake shook his head. "He had a four foot piece of copper pipe pinning him to the seat. Came through the windshield from the semi-truck that jack-knifed, causing the accident and went right through his abdomen."

"Jesus, Jake, I'm sorry."

"He didn't seem to be in any pain." Jake glanced up at Levi, his eyes beginning to well up. "Musta severed his spine, you know? The hood of the car was caved in. I couldn't get inside to sit with him."

"What was his name?" Levi asked.

Jake smiled. "Jimmy… They were traveling to his grandparents for the holiday. I kept him talking, asking him what he was looking forward to eating at Thanksgiving, what he wanted for Christmas… Eventually he stopped answering."

Taking a deep breath, Jake glanced up at the ceiling. "Fuck."

"At least he wasn't alone, right?" Levi asked.

"Fat lot of good that did him," Jake snapped. "Fucking useless, I was."

"That's not fair," Levi said, his tone getting sharp. "That's bullshit and I won't listen to it, Jake Freeman. If you'd have been capable of doing anything you damn well would have, so don't you dare sit here and berate yourself because you aren't capable of ripping through metal with your bare hands."

Jake was staring—eyebrows hitched like he was surprised by that.

"I'm sorry, but you're a good man, Jake. I know you well enough to understand that compulsion to blame yourself, but you didn't cause that accident."

They both sat there for several moments looking at one another, neither of them saying anything.

"He was into Legos," Jake said, folding his arms over his chest, likely hoping to either hold his own emotions in or to prevent Levi from getting any further inside.

"And you're coming with me to Ruby's for dinner," Levi said, holding up a finger when Jake opened his mouth to protest. "You'll do as you're told and you'll like it."

Jake scowled, apparently not a huge fan of being told what to do.

"Don't give me that look," he added. "It's just Chinese food in front of the television with old movies, so you won't even need to talk much if you don't want to."

Jake sat there but didn't say a word.

"Not that anyone can get a word in edgewise when Ruby gets going, anyway."

He cracked a faint hint of a half-smile over that one, which Levi decided was Jake's version of waving the white flag. They each went back to the task at hand, working silently, side by side, with Jake occasionally piping in to give a little background on one of the photos that caught his eye.

It made him sad that Jake was so good when it came to helping others, but complete shit at accepting it from anyone else. He wondered why it was always the people who actually deserved help and support that ended up being the worst at taking it.

Completely pigheaded.

Levi tried holding onto that particular personality flaw, thinking it might ruin Jake for him if he clung to it long enough. Unfortunately, the same quality which would annoy the hell out of him in anyone else managed to seem endearing on Jake.

The bastard.

* * * *

Jake was staring out the passenger side window of Levi's car as they headed back into the city from Ruby's. He'd managed to steal a few minutes alone before they left Julia's and gave his mother a heads-up about Jake's mood and the reason behind it. By the time they'd arrived with more Chinese food than the three of them could ever hope to eat in one sitting, Ruby had gotten herself all dolled up, looking shiny as a brand new penny. Dressed in baggy wool slacks and a big, fuzzy pink sweater, Levi had to admit it was nice seeing her out of her jammies—beautiful as her nightgowns were.

It was evident Ruby was feeling good and she took to monopolizing the conversation the instant they walked through the door. She was like Auntie Mame, blathering on a mile a minute and it wasn't long before she had Jake laughing. She'd used a good chunk of her best material, but entertain the man, she quite successfully did.

About an hour into the second movie, Jake passed out, his head resting on Levi's shoulder. He'd smiled weakly at his mother, able to see it on her face. Ruby knew her son was in love but Levi shook his head at her when she opened her mouth to say something. She didn't need to, for one, because Levi knew exactly what she'd tell him.

Darling, you can't let true love pass you by because of a technicality.

As if Jake's relationship with Voldemort were of little consequence to her.

If Jake truly loves you, you'd be doing him and Voldemort a favor by splitting them up.

Okay, so she wouldn't have referred to Victor by *that* name, but the rest of it was spot on. Unfortunately, from where Levi sat, karma was a two-faced bitch, and while he'd never been a believer in the Bible, that whole do-unto-others bit sounded pretty rational. Jake and Victor might end up splitting up some day, but Levi had zero intentions of ever being the reason for it. He wanted a love which could be given freely and willingly, without condition… not by picking pieces off the carcass of someone else's ruined relationship.

Ruby had scowled at him, as if she'd Jedi mind-tricked her way inside his head and overheard the argument he'd just had with himself.

Sitting silently on the pink suede sofa in his mother's house, Jake had groaned softly, snuggling into Levi a little more closely. Levi had shut his eyes, fully aware that Ruby had been staring a hole into the side of his head yet thankfully kept her opinions to herself. Levi could have stayed like that forever, snuggled up next to Jake, living off unspoken love and what little contact they'd managed to share. Levi had been ashamed of that fact, but not enough to entice him from moving or forcing Jake to move by waking him up—happy to be submerged in the fantasy for as long as it lasted.

The loud blaring of multiple horns and the screeching of tires ripped him from the warm and fuzzy memories of earlier that afternoon. Levi frowned at the rude-ass drivers that sped past them on the highway and he flicked on his turn signal, beginning to steer the car off the freeway toward the midtown exit.

"Feel like getting a drink?" Jake asked, nearly the first words he'd spoken in the last forty minutes. "We could head down to Maxwell's? The piano bar should be open by now."

He checked his side mirror and got back onto the freeway. "Sure, sounds good."

Levi had the feeling Jake needed to not be alone and it made him feel good to be that person for Jake. It took another twenty minutes to get down to the bar, which had a pretty decent sized crowd already, and a fairly rowdy one judging by the sound coming from the room in the back.

He and Jake managed a seat at the massive wooden bar that stretched nearly the entire length of the main room, minus the stage at the back. While technically considered a gay bar, Maxwell's had a varied clientele due to the wide variety of live music featured throughout the week. Thursday nights were popular with the theater geeks due in no small part to the piano bar, which kept the place pretty packed. The bar was adjacent to the theater district, which meant there was never a lack of ridiculously talented entertainers on stage belting out the latest show tune du jour on any given evening. Tonight the crowd was a little lighter thanks to the holiday—many of the students from the universities having gone home to visit family.

They each ordered a beer, though Levi could have used something stronger. He still needed to drive Jake back to midtown and then get himself home after that. He planned on having one beer before switching to water or coffee, deciding this might end up being a long night, after all.

"So, where was Angelo today?" Jake asked.

"Um, home… with his family, I guess," Levi said, thinking the question was an odd one until he remembered they were supposed to be dating.

Jake was grinning, looking a little smug.

Levi didn't particularly appreciate the man tricking him into revealing he'd been lying about the nature of their relationship all this time. *That's what I get for letting my guard down around Jake.*

"For the record, I never bought into the idea the two of you were a couple."

Levi felt his face flush with heat. He started to ask why Jake had been so positive of that fact but decided it was a potential land mine neither of them needed to set off.

"You don't know me, asshole," Levi said, eliciting a chuckle from Jake.

He and Jake each turned, hearing another burst of loud cheers coming from the back.

"What's going on back there?" Jake asked the bartender as he handed each of them their beer.

"Engagement party—an impromptu one from what I hear," he said. "Can I get you two anything else?"

They each shook their heads and he moved down the bar to offer libations to the next group of poor saps who either had nothing better to do for the holiday or were attempting to escape their something-betters in lieu of some fun and frivolity.

"Nice, huh?" Jake asked, nudging his head toward the back room. "Unplanned proposals always seem more romantic, don't you think?"

Levi shrugged. "I don't know, honestly. I seriously doubt that whoever popped the question hadn't already been thinking about it, so realistically, no proposal is likely completely unplanned—discounting Vegas or any other alcohol induced scenario."

Jake's eyebrows rose. "Wow, please try to dial back your romantic optimism."

Laughing, Levi faux-sneered at the man. "I will concede the actual act of proposing might be unplanned, but the thought and act of proposing spontaneously occurring simultaneously? I don't buy it, at least not from anyone in their right mind."

"Just when I think I have you pegged." Jake sighed, staring intently at Levi as he took a swig off his beer.

"Why are you looking at me like that?" Levi asked, beginning to squirm on his bar stool.

"You're so weird." Jake grinned at Levi's reaction. "It's not a bad thing… necessarily."

"You need to work on your delivery, pal," Levi said, with a deadpan expression.

"Apologies, it's just… oh hell, just ignore me, Levi. I'll drink my beer and shut the fuck up."

Levi reached over and took Jake's hand in his. "I'm sorry you're having such a rough week, Jake."

They stared into one another's eyes and for one brief flickering moment, the entire world bled away. Levi became lost in Jake, realizing he would willingly walk away from his own life, his career, his mother… leave behind any and all responsibilities, if doing so meant he could have Jake. It hurt to care for someone so deeply while knowing there could never be a happily-ever-after. Yet Levi couldn't manage to stay away in spite of that. He knew he should, that at some point he would likely have to if he ever intended to have a life and love of his own with someone who was available and thus capable of returning that love. But for now, the thought of not having Jake in his life hurt more than knowing he would never be able to be with him.

"Levi!"

He and Jake both jumped, letting go of one another's hand as they turned to see who was yelling at him. Levi frowned, seeing Dan Cain coming out of the back room, followed by a rather lengthy procession of friends, including David Kramer and Todd Everton. David was visibly intrigued by the company Levi was keeping at the bar and Levi prayed he hadn't seen the whole hand-holding, hypnotizing gaze thing he and Jake had going moments before.

Dan had his arm around the new boyfriend, Kevin, as they approached the bar. Levi forced a smile, thinking how lovely it would be if he never again had to see the man Dan had left Levi for. Getting dumped was never fun, but getting tossed aside for the likes of Kevin the vapid, muscle-twink-from-hell, made the insult sting all the more.

"Levi Goode and… Jake Freeman?" Dan said, looking visibly confused over the fact they were together.

Reminding himself that he didn't actually love Dan anymore never seemed to make the spoonful of betrayal-medicine go down any easier, either—much to Levi's dismay.

"Hello, Dan," Jake said, the tone in his voice sounding less than enthused.

"Here's the man we should be thanking, honey," Dan said, placing a hand on Levi's shoulder while simultaneously laying a disgusting, open-mouthed kiss on Kevin.

The smarmy kiss elicited cheers from the mob of friends who were now surrounding Levi and Jake at the bar.

Levi began to feel himself perspire, trapped and slightly claustrophobic with the wall of people, who currently made any attempt at escaping, futile.

Dan let go of Kevin, then grabbed Levi, planting a *thankfully*, non-open-mouthed kiss on his lips. Dan was visibly lit, eyes glinting as he pulled away, grabbing Levi's wrist and lifting his arm into the air like he'd just been declared the victor in a prize fight.

"Three cheers for the man who single-handedly saved my bacon!" Dan yelled, creating even more of a nuisance of himself.

Mortified when everyone in Dan's party actually gave him a three-cheer shout out, Levi glanced over at Jake apologetically. Seeing that he appeared to be amused by the humiliating ruckus Dan was making made Levi want to slap the smirk right off Jake's face. Even David, who had been Levi's one-true bestie out of all of Dan's friends, was doing nothing to discourage this train wreck.

"We all know how much you treasure your meat," Levi said, flatly.

Dan started laughing hysterically, even hunching over and placing his hands on his knees for a moment. "So funny… Levi, fuck…"

Not exactly the response Levi had been hoping for, deciding he needed to work on his delivery.

"I miss that about you, babe," Dan said, finally settling down.

Levi was praying it was the funny part he missed and not the fuck-part.